A KING UNCAGED

A Historical Novel of Scotland

J R TOMLIN

Albannach Publishing

Chapter One

NOVEMBER 22, 1422

On each side of the path to the high peaked doors of Westminster Abbey, a line of priests stood, swinging censers that wafted streams of incense. They intoned the *Venite* as the solemn train approached. Wisps of smoky incense were whipped away by the sharp November wind.

The voices of the choir seemed to surge through the open west doors. James clasped his hands behind his back as he paced behind a knot of nobles who surrounded the queen as they followed the chariot bearing the coffin. King Henry's long funeral cortege, over land from Vincennes to Rouen, by sea to Dover, and at last to Westminster Abbey in London, was finally, after months, coming to an end. He allowed a silent breath of relief to escape his lips. Behind him, Henry Percy, Earl of Northumberland, was muttering that this could finally be over, and at James' side, his vigilant keeper, Sir William Meryng, gave a sudden shiver when the wind whipped their cloaks.

Harness rattled and hooves clanked on the stone as massive horses heaved, pulling the heavy funeral coach bearing the coffin to the high, peaked doors of the abbey.

Wheels grated with a nerve-shivering sound beneath the swell of solemn music. Even in November's watery sunlight, the silver-gilt effigy atop the coffin shimmered. James craned to glance above. Brilliant ruby and sapphire glass filled the huge windows. The statues of saints set in their niches frowned down upon the long train of nobles who followed the coffin.

Queen Catherine moved rigidly amidst the English royalty, draped in white mourning. The tension between her and the men who would now rule her and the infant king flowed as strongly as the hymns. For a moment, her step faltered, and she sagged as she reached the high, arched doorway. Joan de Beaufort at her side, also in solemn white mourning garb, reached a hand to her elbow. The Duke of Gloucester murmured something to her that James could not make out. A tremble seemed to shake the queen, but she nodded to her good-brother, and they followed the chariot through the towering doors into the cool darkness of the nave.

The scent of beeswax and incense enveloped him as James followed them in. At least they would be out of the wind for the funeral Mass would be long and wearisome. When someone barked a complaint at having his foot was trod upon, James turned his head to see Drummond squeezing his way through the press. James raised an eyebrow at his secretary, who he'd not known had returned from his task in Scotland.

Drummond bowed respectfully when he was close, but his eyes darted toward Meryng. "Your Grace," he said in a low voice so as not to disturb the solemnity of the rising chords of the choir. Surrounded by all the bishops of the realm of England, the thin and frail Archbishop of Canterbury, Henry Chichele, began to intone the requiem mass.

"How went your journey?" James asked in an undertone.

"Sire. I kent you would want your letters as soon as I returned." He drew in a breath. "Especially one from one of your close kin, so I decided not to await your return to your chambers—"

James stilled at the surprise of the words. After a long pause, thinking which of his kin might finally decide he was worth their correspondence, he nodded. "You have it on your person?"

At Drummond's quick nod, James moved toward one of the huge columns. In the press of a thousand nobles, it was impossible to have privacy, but at least he was out of sight of the altar. "You saw Bishop Wardlaw and the Bishop of Glasgow? Delivered the letters?"

"And Thomas Myrton returned with me for your service at their command, especially to keep in close contact with him and with Bishop Wardlaw."

James held out his hand and Drummond slipped a parchment to him. After glancing quickly around to see that no one was taking note of their quiet conversation, James raised his eyebrows at the seal of the earl of Atholl. Close kin indeed, his half-uncle and full brother to that other murderous uncle, the Duke of Albany, who now moldered in a grave.

Holding it close, James slid his thumb under the seal and turned to the column to discretely read it and jerked in a sharp breath at the words. His uncle would throw his influence behind forcing Murdoch Stewart into agreeing to negotiations for James' release from captivity. He folded the letter and slipped it into his sleeve. Leaning a shoulder against the thick marble column, he narrowed his eyes and stared through the wall as though to see his faraway uncle. Atholl... the youngest of his uncles. Atholl had sat by while his older brother committed foul murder and then his nephew allowed

Scotland to descend into lawless chaos. But he still was not an ally to be scorned.

Meryng cleared his throat hoarsely. "Is aught wrong, Lord James?"

James gave the knight a bland smile. "Nae, Sir William. Merely greeting my good secretary after his long journey to and frae Scotland."

When Meryng again turned his face to the high altar, Drummond leaned close. "Myrton carries letters to the English asking safe conduct for Bishop Lauder as well as John Forrester and the Earl of March to come to Pontefract to negotiate terms of your release."

James peered around the column toward the high altar where Joan stood next to the queen. As the Archbishop began another prayer, Joan looked toward James, and their gazes locked. James allowed a smile to touch his lips. He gave a quick nod. She lowered her eyes, but she had seen it.

Oh, James would have a word to say about the negotiations. Beaufort could be won to his cause and his freedom guaranteed. For James had not yet shown his best throw of the die.

He leaned his shoulder against the cool of the marble column and forced himself to patience. He must be patient only a bit longer after the long, weary years past. There would be months of negotiations, of couriers carrying messages and waiting for commissioners of both kingdoms, he was sure. But already he saw greed for his ransom in the eyes of the English—merchants all beneath their finery. Except for Henry. Henry had been a warrior and king through and through. James sent a prayer of thanksgiving the man was dead, might he burn in Hell.

Beaufort would temporize and stall as he tried to squeeze every groat from their dealings. James needed another bribe, a gain Beaufort could not find elsewhere.

The prayers droned and James stifled a sneeze from the smell of the drifting incense. Percy sidled up and nudged James with an elbow. "Damn," Percy muttered. "How long will Beaufort and the Archbishop drag this out?"

James shrugged. "It can nae end soon enough." The drone of the funeral mass flowed past him as he flexed and unflexed his hands. At one point, he pushed the letter further into his sleeve, ensuring it was safe and out of sight. Tugging at his doublet, he bit back a sigh. At last an age later, the mass was over and Henry safely in his tomb.

"Meet me in my chambers," James said to Drummond and shouldered his way through the crowd, out the through doors, and into the cold sunlight. At almost a run, he dashed for his horse. "Lord James," Sir William protested behind him. "Why the unseemly hurry?"

James jerked his reins free and threw himself into his saddle. Months of delay were behind him. More lay ahead, but he would be acting, forcing the issue finally. He would make sure he was never again a pawn in another's hands. He put his heels to his horse's flanks and set it to a trot through the crowd as Meryng cursed behind him.

By the time he reached Windsor, the sky was darkening. In the bailey, he tossed his reins to a stable boy and hurried to his chamber in a minor wing of the palace. A servant was prodding a fire in the hearth. James motioned the man out, sat, and pulled parchment and quill to him, checked the nib, and dipped it in ink when Meryng stomped into the doorway, still muttering under his breath. James gave him a politic smile. "No one but my own people is to disturb me today. There has been no time to see to my affairs, and they press."

The knight glowered at him as he withdrew, shouting for a squire to guard the door as he went.

Drummond was panting as he motioned the stocky newcomer to their company, Thomas Myrton, ahead of him.

When the door was firmly closed, Drummond said, "You are writing your own letters, Your Grace?"

"This one, I am." James chewed his lower lip for a moment as he examined Myrton. If Wardlaw trusted the man, then James would as well. "The import is such they should be in my own hand. You will both carry them to speed matters as much as can be. I am proposing..." He leaned back in his chair and twitched a smile. "I will propose that I take a lady of the English court, one of the highest degree, as my bride to be crowned Queen of Scots as soon as I regain my kingdom."

Drummond's eyebrows rose, he opened his mouth, and then closed it.

"Gold frae Scotland they will welcome for my ransom, but withal their need is nae so great that it will hurry the matter. So I must offer something that Beaufort will esteem as much as gold. I can offer a crown." He bent over his parchment and began to write. "You'll leave with them at first light on the morn."

At Drummond's sigh, James looked up and smiled. "I am a hard taskmaster. But home is in sight, my friend. It is worth a weary trip, you ken."

James smiled a little as he pretended not to hear when Drummond muttered, "But I thought when I became a priest it would be my knees that got weary and not my arse."

But then James looked up, growing serious again, "Dinnae think I'll forget how much I owe you. All of you."

Iain of Alway gave Drummond a scathing look from where he was bent over a chest of their clothing, still folded away from the long trip from France. "We do no more than our duty."

James sucked his teeth for a moment as he puzzled over a response to his uncle's letter. The importance of his help in forcing the regent to accept James' return couldn't be understated, but the sudden turnaround made James suspicious. How much could he trust the offer? He gratefully accepted it, but in his letter to Bishop Wardlaw, he tried to delicately hint at taking care with such a new ally. But the most important matter he took his time phrasing: *Propose I offer a truce and to guarantee the truce that I take a suitable lady of their court as my bride to be crowned as my queen.* At last he pressed his ring into the soft wax of the seal on the last letter and looked up. "It grows late, and I desire a walk in the east park, Iain." When his squire gave him a questioning look, James continued, "And I must do so privily...with no guards about."

Though the watch over James to prevent his escape had eased slightly since King Henry died, privacy was difficult to come by, so Iain frowned as he thought the matter over. "I heard Meryng call one of the squires to keep watch when he left. How...?" He shook his head. "Mayhap I could distract him?"

"Aye, but so much that he would not notice my slipping out?" He eyed Drummond, who was at least close to his own size though much less muscled. It would be too humiliating to be caught impersonating a priest, but perhaps merely wearing the priest's cloak would suffice. The guards had seen his household come and go often enough not to question seeing one of them—if they thought it was Drummond. He stood and held out a hand. "Give me your cloak." It was a slight disguise, but if the guards didn't look too closely—

"Iain, pretend to be sneaking out. Tell him you're meeting a kitchen maid and spin a story. Make it a good one."

Iain pressed a hand to his chest with a smirk. "My lord, would I have such a tale to spin?" He was out the door before James could give him a rap on the head.

After making sure his distinctive auburn hair was well covered by the hood, James opened the door. Iain was standing, laughing, at a far turn of the hall and motioning to describe a generous female shape. James turned his back and strode firmly in the opposite direction and took a winding path to the kitchen gate.

The park was dark with shafts of light from castle windows. It was vast, towering trees spread in the distance and soft grass underfoot. Under the first of the trees a dark-cloaked figure stood. She held out her hand. "Come, my lord, for I soon will be missed."

He only kissed her hand, for he was in no state for words.

"This way." She tugged his hand to lead him along a narrow path. "You were careful, I hope."

"Careful," he choked. "You are a fine one to speak of care, chancing sending me a note by a servant."

Her chime of laughter drifted on the cooling evening breeze. Stepping off the path into the denser darkness beneath the canopy of trees, she said, "Here at least we can be alone, if not in any comfort. We can safely speak, so tell me, I beg. The news from Scotland? It is good? Your couriers returned."

"Better news than we expected. The Earl of Atholl, my uncle...my half-uncle, will help me wrest power away frae the regent. But more importantly—" He smiled and brushed his fingers along her soft cheek. "My delight, I gave orders that part of the agreement must be that a bride will return with me when I return home."

He reached out to grasp her arms through her cloak. "I dinnae have words for speech. Too long..." He pulled her to him and kissed her neck within the hooded cloak, her cheeks, and at last her lips, but she turned her lips. "It has been too long since I held you."

She leaned into him for a moment before she turned her head away. "We have no time, James," she gasped.

He moaned. "I ken. Joan..." He murmured her name,

savoring it as he could not her. "Joan, my heart. I need you. If I'm to rule, I need you beside me. You will truly marry an uncrowned king? Though your family despises me?"

She huffed a little breath and ran her fingertips over his face. "They will not when you have your crown. You know that. Another royal line in our family will not be despised. I will do anything, James, to help you win back to Scotland. I will twist my uncle to my will if I must. I swear it. He dotes on me if less than Henry did. If your ambassadors suggest it, and I tell him it is my will...for it is, love. Yes, Joan de Beaufort will wed James Stewart of Scotland. And only death can part us."

She shivered and he pulled his cloak around her.

"It isn't cold," she said thoughtfully and twined her arms around his waist. "It is hope that goes through me. We have a life to go to, and I am keen to reach it."

He leaned his forehead against hers. "I cannot promise you an easy life, my love. I was born to trouble and return to it. I would I could make such a promise."

He turned his gaze past her into the dark trees, and past them he saw across the moorlands and the mountains, over rivers of his childhood, beside the streams he had crossed long years ago fleeing from death at the hands of his own family.

Chapter Two

Pontefract Castle was a fearsome place. James could only be thankful that all he knew of the dark and oppressive network of dungeons hollowed out of the bedrock thirty-five feet below the castle was rumor. But the castle itself was oppressive enough, a vast stone fortress within a series of curtain walls that formed two outer baileys surrounding the high, massive keep.

At least the stone walls eight and ten feet thick or more in places gave relief from summer's heat. But within these walls he could not sleep. Perhaps it was that freedom was too near, but he swore that when freedom was his, no castle would contain him. The walls pressed in like the brazen bull of the ancient Greeks.

During the long summer night he went over the last verse of his work, The King's Book he called it. Perhaps he should give it an elaborate name, but just his book was how he thought of it, and the end was at last in sight as he wrote the final verses.

Thanks might be — and fair in love befall —
The nightingale that with so good intent

Sang there of love, the notes sweet and small,
Where my heart's fair lady was,
Gladdened her before she further went.
And thou, my gillyflower, must thanked be
All other flowers for the love of thee!

The negotiators for the English, the bishops of Durham and Worcester, the Earl of Westmoreland, and Sir Thomas Chaworth kept to the great hall, where they stood or sat, played cards or dice, and grumbled over the delay. Durham wrote long lists of what James was not sure and every two days another letter arrived from Henry Beaufort with documents that the English added to their pile. James pretended to ignore them. He wouldn't lower himself to negotiate like a merchant at the fair for his own release. Only Henry Percy, also one of the negotiators, was welcome company.

Percy was happy enough to ride out to the hunt during the early morning. They galloped through thick woods, the only sound birdsong and the thud of their horses' hooves, trailed by a dozen servants in Percy's livery. They pulled up, and in the silence, it became evident that something had been there before them. The earth was gouged and pushed aside, the leaves freshly crushed. The roots of the beech trees were scored and cratered where some creature had slashed the earth. Bluebells sprawled where they'd been ripped up. Percy called for their heavy boar lances, thick enough to withstand such a beast's weight.

"It shan't have gone far yet," James said.

A few minutes later they cornered a huge boar, easily twice the weight of any man, with tusks as long as James' forearm. Dismounted, they both planted their lance butts on the ground. James stared into tiny, golden eyes filled with fury at their encroachment. It bellowed and charged. He held onto his lance for his life when it hit, jarring him to his teeth. His arms shook, and he desperately fought to keep to his feet.

The lance was sank deep in the boar's chest, but the creature shook its head, blood spraying as it tried to rip him with its tusks. Henry shouted for permission to finish it and James shouted back, "By the Holy rood, aye!"

Percy ran at the boar and flung his whole weight to force his lance through its neck.

When it fell, its weight jerked both of them on top of it. James' laugh was a little shaky when he scrambled to his feet and wiped splatters of blood from his face. The servants heaved the boar onto a pack horse.

Percy slapped James' shoulder, and they shared deep drinks from a wine bag before they mounted and headed back for the castle. When they rode out of the shadows of the first gate, the bailey yard was full of upheaval and noise. Chests and boxes were being unloaded from wagons. Men-at-arms were shouting. Horses were being unsaddled and led to the stables.

A nobleman in black, dust-covered armor and surcoat was standing in the middle shouting commands. Myrton stood beside him.

"At last, they must have arrived. Now we can finish this business." Percy jumped from the saddle and tossed his reins to a stable boy. "Have that boar taken to the kitchens. We worked for that meat."

James snorted. "I thought for a moment I might not live to be crowned after all." He nodded to Percy, who was turning to head for the castle. But he had to agree. At last...

He strode toward the nobleman, frowning. And then he laughed, carried back years and climbing to the top of Bass Rock, to a boy teaching him to roast birds' eggs and watching the flight of ten thousand gannets. Robert Lauder. There were a few speckles of gray in his hair now, but it was he without doubt.

Robbie turned when he heard James' laugh and dashed

forward. A few feet away he sank onto his knees to kiss James' hand. "Your Grace."

"Robert Lauder." Another laugh broke from James' chest. He urged Lauder to his feet. "By all that's holy, it's a delight to see your face. And now lord of Edrington and Bass, they say."

Robbie Lauder's face was split with a wide grin, and he was shaking his head in evident wonder. "As foolish as it sounds, I somehow expected to see the boy I once kent."

James threw his arms wide. "Not quite." He looked around at the chaos of the yard. "Where are the others?"

"I told them I'd oversee the unloading while they prepared for meeting the English. I prefer to see things done aright. My brother is eager to speak with you before the negotiations begin."

"As I am to him. Who else came?"

"James Douglas of Belvenie, Abbot Patrick of Cambuskenneth, Sir Patrick Dunbar of Bele, John Hales and Archdeacon Borthwick of Glasgow."

"So Dunbar stayed away." James nodded thoughtfully. The man was too close to Murdoch to trust, so he'd hardly be missed. Then he paused to look his old friend over from head to foot and was shaken again by a short laugh. "I too thought of you still as a lad. You gladden my eyes, Robbie. Truly you do."

Robert motioned to Myrton. "Oversee that our men are properly barracked, Myrton, and I'll show His Grace to my brother."

Within the castle, they climbed the stairs and entered the solar unannounced, to find the bishop standing by a narrow window for the little breeze. That Robert and the bishop were brothers was evident in a glance. William Lauder, only a decade older than James, was tall and thin with piercing blue eyes and a beak of a nose, but in spite of his fine robes, he looked worn and weary, his face thin and cheeks hallow. He was alone, for which James was thankful. They had much to discuss, and the others were too close to Murdoch to be trusted.

"Your Grace." Bishop Lauder grasped James' hand to kiss it and James gripped his arm.

"You had a weary trip, I fear."

"Somewhat, but that matters not. What matters is that we wrung permission to negotiate from Murdoch. Though he and his sons and other nobles are afeart what might come of your return, and well might they be. Eighteen years first Albany and now Murdoch and his friends have had to pick Scotland clean like buzzards on a corpse."

James gave a sharp nod. "I've had your letters and Wardlaw's. This is no news to me. But if there's to be a reckoning, first I must return home."

Bishop Lauder wiped his face that had paled, and James realized the man needed to sit. The long journey from Glasgow had obviously wearied him beyond his strength, so James sat and waved the two to chairs. "Indeed. Murdoch is more incompetent by the day, and no one can control his sons. It's impossible to tell you which of them is worse."

"Have you seen the English demands?" Robbie asked.

"They mentioned seventy thousand English pounds, and I told them that we cannot possibly meet so large a payment, not even in payments over several years. The English are ready to sell me like a plump goose at market, but I cannot bargain with them myself. It would hardly be seemly. I know that the Bishop of Durham has sums of the cost of my..." James clenched his jaw. "Of my keep in their so kind care these eighteen years. I believe they will lessen their demands to the total of that, but every item must be pursued because their greed will see no bounds. Of that you may be sure. Forbye they'll want hostages as surety."

The bishop nodded thoughtfully. "Have they proffered a list?"

"Not to me, and it seems to me that we could offer them one. Forbye, it could be one to our advantage," James said with a smile. "If we are to have a number of our nobles in English hands, I'd see that as few as can be should be my allies and as many my enemies as possible."

"Bishop Wardlaw had thought of that and we put together a list, not too obviously favoring your allies but with many who have robbed your treasury and profited from your absence. I have such a list ready to offer."

James' smile widened. "And when it comes to paying the ransom, I'll be in no great hurry to see the return of my enemies."

Robbie laughed. "A wise policy, Sire."

"They also want a truce and no more troops to be sent to France. If, as I heard, the Douglas and Buchan are raising a new army to take to France that may prove a problem."

"We expected that. Suppose we only guarantee that once you are in your kingdom, the truce goes into effect and no more troops are to leave. You can hardly be expected to prevent departures whilst you are in England, after all. With the offer of a seven-year truce both at land and sea, that should suffice, although at first I will offer only four years, which they would never agree to."

"They are hard bargainers. Be prepared for them to try to wring every groat and concession, but—" James gazed through the slit window into the bright afternoon sun. "Aye, I believe if you make it appear we are conceding much and reluctantly, they will agree. And Bishop Beaufort has already agreed—most privily—that the sum of my bride's dowry will be deducted from my ransom, though the dowry is almost shamefully low for so great a lady."

"Beaufort?" Robbie leaned his elbows on his knees to look more closely at James.

"It is agreed between the two of us that if you ask for a marriage treaty between me and an English lady of royal stock, they will agree to discuss my will in the matter, which he kens well. So he told me he has instructed the negotiators."

"A lady has been named between you, then?" Bishop Lauder asked. "And he has agreed?"

"Aye. Indeed it has. And he has."

Chapter Three

FEBRUARY 12, 1424

J oan smoothed the skirt of her gown, the comeliest she had ever owned. Everything she wore was new. Her smock was of fine linen, the under-gown of the finest wool to protect against February's chill. Of a deep sapphire blue as her mother had insisted, it was snug to her hips and then flared to the ground. The outer surcoat, a paler blue, was samite with shimmering gold thread running through; its deep V-neck showed the darker gown beneath.

Queen Catherine was officially helping her to dress but seemed to look through them as though they weren't there. The queen turned and wandered to the window. Pulling a comb through her hair one last time, Joan's mother smoothed it down her back to her waist. She made a little smacking sound with her lips and said, "Soon I may never see you again, daughter."

Joan turned and pressed a quick kiss to her mother's cheek, but she had no idea what to say.

"I have no right to be sad." Her mother shook her head and smiled, although it looked a bit false. "How many mothers have their daughters with them so long?"

"They tried to convince me to marry enough times. Now I think my uncle may now be glad of my being such the stubborn girl he always called me."

Her mother shook out her veil, silk so fine it seemed no more than a wisp. "Henry was too fond to force you." Her marriage had been fiercely argued since she was fourteen and her betrothed died. Then Joan swore they'd have to drag her screaming to the altar. She'd thought a few times that Henry might do so, but he'd given way to her entreaties. Joan lowered her head so the veil could be settled over her hair and a narrow gold circlet put on her brow to hold it in place. Her mother kissed her forehead. "Beautiful daughter. They'll love you, but—" her voice broke. "Sending you to live with the wild Scots. It is a hard thing."

Leaving behind the civilized ways of the English was frightening enough that when she allowed herself to consider it, her heart beat like mad, but James would be with her. All would be well. She was sure of it. She held her mother's hand and turned to look into the mirror that her little sister, Margaret, was holding up for her, eyes wide. "You look so elegant, Joan. I hope I look so when I wed."

"You will, Meg." In the mirror, her mouth curved into a smile. Meg was right that she looked elegant. She squeezed her mother's hand. "All will be well. I promise."

She hardly felt the stairs under her feet as she hurried down to the bailey yard. Her father should have been the one to lead her mount to the church, but he was long dead and her two elder brothers prisoners in France, so it was her youngest brother Edmund, a rangy boy of eighteen, still with a few spots on his sullen face, who lifted her by the waist and seated her in the saddle. The cream-colored mare was a wedding gift from her uncle. It was a beauty, and she touched its mane that was braided with sprigs of lily, bishop's lace, and roses.

"Ready?" Edmund scowled up at her.

She touched his shoulder. "Don't be so angry." She couldn't help that it had been the Scots who had captured their brothers in France. It seemed unfair for him to blame James, and they had little time left to make peace. "Can't you be happy for me?"

"Are you? Happy?" he said as he took the bridle and led the way through the gate and onto the street.

"I am." She smiled up at the watery February sunlight. The throng that lined the London Bridge was cheering as the mare pranced daintily across. Banners flapped overhead, held up by the men-at-arms, marching in a line on each side of the party; the queen, her mother, and other guests followed. The veil made the world look hazy and dreamlike.

Beneath the massive square bell tower, the grounds of the Church of St. Mary Overie bustled with the people of London, happy to cheer for a royal wedding, even that of a Scot. James stood before the arched doors, shining like a Roman god in his cloth-of-gold doublet beneath a cloak of crimson velvet blazoned with the Lion Rampant of Scotland. Beside him stood her uncle, Henry Beaufort, the bishop. A rushing sound in her ears pulsed in a strange counterpoint to the shouts.

His face solemn, James strode forward to meet her as Edmund lifted her down from the saddle. He took her hand to lead her to the doors where they would be wed, in the open as was custom so the crowd could witness their joining. Everything seemed even hazier, and time heaved oddly along while her stomach fluttered as though filled with riotous butterflies. The buzz in her head confused the words of the ceremony. She could barely follow what James said in response to her uncle, but then it was her turn. She took a deep, calming breath. She swallowed hard and managed to keep her voice even to say, "I, Joan de Beaufort, take thee,

James Stewart, to my wedded husband, to have and to hold from this day forward, for better, for worse, for richer, for poorer, in sickness and in health, till death us depart, according to God's holy ordinance. And thereto I pledge thee my troth."

The bishop took the ring and said a quick prayer over the gold band with its square emerald. James retrieved it from him and lifted her left hand. Her head spun, and she sucked in a breath. She would not faint at her wedding and have her new husband think her a weak goose.

"With this ring I thee wed: This gold and silver I thee give, with my body I thee worship, and withal my worldly goods I thee endow." He slipped the ring a little way onto each finger, saying in turn, "In the name of the Father, the Son, and the Holy Spirit." With the last phrase, he slid it onto her ring finger.

Cheers and whistles nearly drowned out her uncle's closing blessing. People surged forward and a fresh-faced acolyte held up an alms bowl. James slipped his arm around her waist, and she welcomed the support as she scooped up a handful of silver pennies. She suddenly felt giddy and a laugh bubbled up. She flung the coins to scatter them into the crowd. They shouted her name and scrambled for the coins. James flung a handful high over the heads of the mob. She grabbed more and tossed them until the bowl was empty. She smiled up at James, and through the mist of her veil she saw him look down at her, his large, piercing blue eyes shining.

She couldn't help softly laughing as James led her into the church.

Quickly as the wedding had passed, the Mass dragged as though time had slowed to a crawl. In the cool darkness of the church, she breathed in the pleasant scent of beeswax candles and frankincense and tried not to twitch with impatience. While her uncle droned on through the service, her mind wandered to the banquet that awaited them. Was the food sufficiently elegant? Her mother had assured her it was. Had they planned enough minstrels and tumblers? Later, for the first time since returning from France, she and James would at last be alone, and the thought made her heart race. The bedding revels were less to her taste. Poor Queen Catherine had been near tears at the shouts and rude instructions when Henry's companions tossed him into bed with her. Still, it must be borne for what came after.

At one point, her uncle read from the scripture of Ruth: "Do not be against me, as if I would abandon you and go away; for wherever you will go, I will go, and where you will stay, I will stay. Your people are my people..." It jerked Joan's mind back into the dimness of the church. Ruth had gone to an alien land. Joan was no Bible scholar, but that she remembered. Ruth had taken strangers as her people. Suddenly, she felt cold at the thought of a life amongst people she didn't know who might hate her. James must have felt her tremble, for he pressed her fingers. She took a deep breath. James' people would be hers. She was sure of it. She must be brave and strong.

Chapter Four

They rode side by side to Bishop Beaufort's Southwark Palace, a short ride from the church for the wedding feast. James could not keep his eyes off Joan, though he tried not to be too obvious. A man besotted was considered shameful, but how could it not be seen? He had been besotted since the first day he saw her walking below his window in the garden of Windsor.

He took her on his arm into the great hall beneath beams of afternoon sun let in through the enormous, high rose window.

Pages scampered, strewing a scattering roses petals before them. Henry Beaufort, now out of his vestments for the Mass, had donned fine, deep-purple velvet robes. For the first time in his life, he bowed to James with a smile that James found grotesque and said, "Welcome, Your Grace." He took his niece's hand and kissed it. Then he ceremoniously led them onto the dais and to the seats of honor at its center. Queen Catherine embraced Joan and kissed her on each cheek. Young Edmund did as well, although he looked as though he had bitten into a sour pomegranate. But young

Margaret was bouncing on her toes as she hurried to fiercely hug her sister. No one was so eager to embrace James. Welcoming the Scot they had so long despised seemed a draught of bitter medicine from the looks on their faces.

After a fraught moment, his new good mother, Lady Margaret, took each of his hands and leaned forward to kiss him on the cheek. "Your Grace," she murmured. James brushed fingers over his moustache to hide a smirk at their pain at being forced to finally give him his proper address.

When he and Joan had taken their seats, Bishop Beaufort remained standing to give his blessing to the feast. James remembered that the bishop didn't usually drone on forever over it because he had been much too nervous to break his fast earlier and feared soon his stomach might grumble. He glanced at Joan, who was smiling thoughtfully at her hands folded modestly in her lap, and wondered if she had been nervous as well. He had felt her tremble several times, but her voice had been steady for the vows. Lady Margaret was at his side, and the thought of managing a long conversation with her would have soured the feast, but surely he could be forgiven for concentrating on his new bride.

He realized the bishop was looking at him with his caterpillar-like eyebrows raised. He must have completed the blessing. James stood and held out his goblet to be filled. "To Lady Joan, my bride, soon Queen of the Scots!"

Everyone jumped to their feet. "Lady Joan!" the filled hall shouted. "Lady Joan! Lady Joan!" Hundreds of goblets rang together. James emptied his cup and had it refilled. Sitting, he put it into Joan's hands to share with her. A sly smile curved her lips as she turned it to drink from the same place his lips had touched, and his face heated. This feast would last hours, but it couldn't be over soon enough for him. At last, he would be alone with his bride.

While pipers and fiddlers took up a gay tune, servants

carried in roast goose for the first course. Since the wine was quickly going to James' head, as soon as he offered Joan the best slice off his knife, he dug in. Then he remembered there would be many more courses to come, so he leaned back and watched Joan laughing as she leaned forward to trade a quip with Henry Percy further down the dais. Dutifully, he turned to Lady Margaret on the other side. She looked glum, and he wondered if it was only that she had always despised him.

Courses of venison, partridge, and fresh salmon followed, each course crowned with an elaborate subtlety. There was a sugar modeled into a castle with moat, nestling doves, and a ship under full sail. With so many of the English court either fighting in France or some prisoner there, many faces were missing, but they weren't ones James missed, but Joan must. She would have no chance to say farewell to her brothers. James motioned for her cup to be filled with honey mead, and she absently sipped. She was sparkling with gaiety, laughing at the tumblers who were chasing a one of their number dressed as a pig around the tables. But he squeezed her fingers anyway, and she smiled at him from the corner of her eyes. Finally, and James thought it must have been hours, the trumpets blew and dozens of servants scuttled out to clear the trestle tables.

Once the tables, except the one on the dais, were cleared, the doors were flung open and servants wheeled in a great pie, three feet across with a luscious brown crust, to push it in a slow progress up the length of the hall. The guests shouted and clapped as it went. Two men followed, each with a brown sparrowhawk on his gauntleted arm.

James leaned close to Joan and whispered, "This will be unruly, my love. But we could turn it to our advantage if you like. If you would prefer a quiet to the bedding revels, that is..." He raised his eyebrows, for he wasn't sure what she would prefer.

"I've no great taste for them. But how so?"

"When I rise to go cut open the crust, make your way to the doors." James grinned. "Once they loose the hawks, I wager no one will watch what we are doing for at least a few moments."

Bishop Beaufort stood and bowed, motioning for James to take the honor, so James put a bit of swagger in his stride as he went to meet the pie below the dais. James drew his sword with a flourish. He lifted it high, held it for a moment, and then swung it down. The crust shattered. Two dozen white doves flapped into the air with a burst of squeaks and coos, feathers flying as the birds tried to escape into the rafters. More laughter and cheers went up from the guests who lined the walls and crowded the doorway four deep, drowning out the lively tune coming from the gallery. "Release them," James shouted to the falconers.

The hawks burst from the falconers' arms and soared into the air, circled, swooped through the rafters in pursuit of their prey. There was utter chaos with doves dashing against the windows to try to escape while the onlookers shouted wagers and cheered when one of the hawks plunged in to take a dove with a welter of flying feathers and speckles of blood to loud applause. As feathers drifted down, James darted through the crowd into the doorway where Joan stood, nervously chewing her lip. He grabbed her hand and pulled her into the corridor. "Haste you," he said, smothering laughter, "before we are missed. They'll soon be after us like the hawks on the doves."

Joan gathered her skirts in her hands and dashed beside him down the corridor and for the stairs. He snatched her arm and hustled her up the steps. They had barely set foot at the top when James heard a shout and laughter from below. "After them," came a shout that James was sure was Henry Percy. James cursed and shoved a panting Joan ahead of him toward the door to their chamber. By then he could hear hoots, whistles, and laughter from their pursuers. James jerked the door open, thrust Joan inside, and slammed the door. He was laughing so hard he had to lean his head against the wood as he dropped the bar into place. There was a thud and hammering.

Joan sank into a chair giggling and covered her mouth with her hands.

"Damn you, James Stewart, open the door," Percy shouted, and there were catcalls.

"He doesn't want to admit he doesn't know how to sheath his sword!" someone else taunted.

"I'll bed my own bride," James shouted back. He turned to Joan, still laughing. A second later they were in each other's arms. Joan's mouth was tender and tasted of honey mead. James was sure he would grow to love the taste of mead on her tongue, and he loved the feel of her soft arms around him. He kissed her deeply, running his hand through the cascading fall of her honey-blonde hair, and tightened his arms around her. She shifted so she could pillow her head against his shoulder.

"I think," giddy, Joan began to giggle, "that I am tipsy with happiness."

He put his lips to the pulse in her throat. With his free hand he began unfastening her lacings. "My heart's desire..." he murmured against her skin.

"I feel as though all the bone and blood in me is no more than a feather, and if you didn't anchor me with your touch, that I would float away." She shivered when his lips brushed her ear and his tongue traced a path up its curve.

"Forbye," James said with a smile, "I'll have no floating away on our wedding night."

Suddenly serious, she whispered, "Where you will stay, I

will stay...tonight and every night..." Looking up at him, her eyes were so soft and glowing, showing nothing but trust, that James caught his breath.

"You shan't ever regret our marriage, Joan," he promised. "I swear it by all that is holy."

Chapter Five

APRIL 5, 1424

They rode at a steady pace, at James insistence, stopping only to allow the horses to drink and Joan to rest and stretch the cramps from her legs. She rode near at his side, companionable as she pointed out birds and flowers she hadn't seen in the south. Henry Percy ofttimes rode beside them with their escort strung out for a mile behind them, and his old friend's jibes about James missing the English court began to fray at his temper. Behind the long train of men-at-arms and the nobles, sent more for Joan's honor than his, chattered like magpies above the clank of harness and plod of hundreds of hooves.

Freedom was before him. The desire to hurry burned in him like a fire, but he pressed it down. When he saw the band of the River Tweed stretched through the green valley, its wide turquoise waters rippling with silver in the May sunlight, James drew up his horse and raised his hand for a halt. Grass grew thick in the shallows that edged the ford. A brown adder basked on a log in the sunshine and raised its head before slithering out of sight in the reeds. A golden eagle flew in lazy swoops overhead.

On a hill beyond the river haugh, a thin tendril of smoke rose and twisted, but the scent on the air was of thyme and heather and the river gave up a faint gurgle.

"My lord, are you all right?" Joan asked.

He nodded, his throat closed up so tight he could not speak, for beyond the Tweed, Scotland was laid out before him. First lay a checkered range of pastures and meadows that slowly rose to braes dappled with green and yellow and purple heather and jasmine and patches of gorse. A dozen miles away, clear in that spring sunlight, the purple Lammermuirs rimmed the rich Scotland sky.

James struggled for a breath against the tight band that had formed, squeezing him, almost as much grief and the lost years as joy at the sight of...home. He reached a hand for Joan's blindly, for he wouldn't turn so that others would see the tears that leaked from his eyes. He cleared his throat roughly, shamed at his weakness.

Joan's horse whickered, and he felt her as she nudged her mount closer and squeezed his fingers. "Look," she said. "There are people gathered beyond. In Scotland."

He rubbed his eyes with the heel of his hand, pretending there had been no tears.

"At last," Percy announced as he thudded up at a canter. "My duty is done once we cross the Tweed. I've kept my oath to the chancellor to deliver you safely to Scotland."

The bands squeezing his chest released at last as James sucked in a great breath of the moist river air. A laugh welled up, surprising him. "Indeed, my old friend. So you have." He turned his head as the sound of bells reached him, he wasn't sure from whence, but a joyful carillon and then deeper, steady tolls joined them, carried on the breeze. "So let us be about it. There is one more river to cross."

Joan's bright gaze caught his. She bent her head in submission, but her eyes sparkled as she said, "At your command, my king."

James grinned and put his heels to his horse's flanks. "Home!" he shouted. His horse caught his excitement and took off down the slope with an arm-wrenching plunge. The chime of Joan's laugh mixed with music of the pealing bells and the splash of the river as he crossed, but he heard her horse splash into the river behind him.

He felt as though he might choke on the joy as he pulled up his prancing, plunging mount in front of the shouting, cheering host of bishops in finery along with abbots and nobility, with commonality around the edges of the crowd. "The king!" they shouted. "It's the king!" He jumped from the saddle and rushed to catch Joan's bridle. He swung her down to put her on her feet. She was gasping with the fast ride and her laughter. He took both her slender hands in his.

Turning, he gazed at the hundreds of faces around them, slowly shaking his head. So many strangers, who should have been friends, should have been known to him, all of them.

But his heart lurched in his chest with a desire. He sank slowly to his knees and bent. He plunged his hands into the heather to pull it away and pressed his lips to the raw earth. He kissed his native soil and took a deep breath of its sweet smell. When he raised his eyes, Joan was kneeling beside him, her gaze solemn.

As he knelt there, an old man in the purple robes of a bishop stepped out of the crowd. His hair was gray and his face thinner than James' childhood memory, but there was no mistaking Henry Wardlaw, Bishop of St. Andrews. The bishop raised his hands and the cheers faded away.

In a voice deep as the ocean that boomed like breakers on the shore, he intoned, "Welcome home, my king." Then, holding out his hands in blessing, he gave thanks in the words of a Psalm, "Quia apud Dominum misericordia: et copiosa apud eum redemptio. Et ipse redimet Israel, ex omnibus iniquitatibus eius. Gloria Patri, et Filio, et Spiritui Sancto. Amen."

James gave Joan his hand and helped her as they both rose, but he was shaking his head at the sight of his old tutor and mentor. He reached his free hand to grasp the bishop's. "Your Reverence." His voice broke. "To see you again."

Bishop Wardlaw beamed. "The joy of welcoming you home, my son, I cannot express it." He turned his gaze to Joan. "And your bride."

"I forget myself. My lady, this is my beloved tutor and father in God, Bishop Wardlaw of St. Andrews and Primate of the realm. Come himself to greet us."

Joan gave a sweeping curtsy. "Most Reverend Father."

James turned at someone saying his name. "I am another here who remembers you well, Your Grace, though after these years..." The man who greeted James so was in his fifties and yet appeared fit as a man much younger. He was tall with long legs and broad shoulders. His head was bald, so smooth that James thought it must be shorn, as was the man's face except for his moustache, a thicket of wiry auburn hair that reached nearly to his jaw. His piercing eyes were a pale blue. When James frowned in puzzlement, the man bent a knee and said, "It is no wonder you dinnae remember me. It has been too many years, Sire."

"Many years indeed, my lord," James said coolly. He couldn't afford to offend this man, but warmth was truly beyond him.

"I swear to you that my brother's actions and Murdoch's were none of my doing. If any action of mine would have freed you sooner—"

James waved away his uncle's protests, which he supposed might be true. How much he could trust Atholl remained to be seen, but he might be telling the truth. "All in the past, uncle, and I hope you will ride with us to Scone." He smiled and wondered if it looked as false as it felt. "But you have not met my lady wife."

Though there were many who needed greeting, he spotted Walter Giffard and motioned the man who had been his main companion in imprisonment for so many years to his side, before he turned to Henry Percy, who was frowning as he was ignored amongst the crowd. "I owe you an oath, my lord, and I hereby give it. The provisions of the treaty will be kept, and I swear to honor the truce between our kingdoms as well as pay the ransom agreed on."

Percy gave him a formal bow. "You will send the treaty under your great seal for me to forward?"

At James' nod, Percy turned and strode back to his horse. Under his own banner, Percy splashed across the wide River Tweed to rejoin the armed troop that awaited his return.

James signaled to Iain to lead his horse to him. First he lifted Joan by her waist onto her mount before he swung into the saddle. He drew his sword and displayed it before he rested it before him. Slowly he spread his gaze across the waiting crowd, most notably lacking the great lords of the realm. Nowhere were the Douglases or Murdoch Stewart in the crowd. As he looked from face to face, a silence fell over the people beneath the sound of tolling bells.

He stood in his stirrups and raised his voice. "Hear me. The rapine in my kingdom will end. My royal coffers are empty, and too many of my nobles are but a pack of wolves devouring the people like sheep. But I will bring the rule of law to the land." He took a deep breath. "If God grant me but the years of a dog, I swear to you that whilst I live, the key will keep the lock and the bracken hedge the cow."

There was a rustling, and James saw in the darting eyes a deep doubt that he could keep such an oath.

Chapter Six

The scent of Scotland was strong in his nostrils, and James found it strange that what he remembered most, now that he was once again home, was the smell of earth and river and plants. The crowd had formed into a long cavalcade, and they rode through the meadows, grain fields, and pastures of the green Merse, ranging alongside the River Tweed. With Joan beside him, he pointed out stone towers of knights and churches as they passed. As urgent as it was for him to be crowned, he needed to immerse himself in the feel of his homeland and share it with his bride, so he led them in a leisurely ride westward until they would swing north toward Scone.

The afternoon sun was high in the sky when Robert Lauder urged his horse beside James. The lion banner flapped overhead in a slight breeze. A chunky red finch fluttered across their path to disappear into a patch of trees. Lauder cleared his throat. "A word if I might, Your Grace."

"Of course." James smiled. "I have to remember you're a man grown and not call you Robbie. I remember our days as lads too well. I was sorry when I heard of your father's death. I should have mentioned it sooner."

"I need to...feel you should see a village over yon." Lauder shifted in the saddle, and he gave James an uneasy look from the corner of his eyes. "We could take a small party whilst your good lady and the others rest just ahead."

There was a shady copse of birches a few minutes' ride ahead on a heathery slope. "Your words when you arrived, that you would bring law to the lands. Braw words, Your Grace, but I'd show you what you face."

James gave a sharp nod and motioned for a man-at-arms. Joan was murmuring a protest at being left behind. James helped her from her saddle and leaned close. "Please me, my lady, by staying safely here. Until I ken better what we face, I'd take no risks." She squeezed his hand, but hers was trembling, so he motioned to Walter Giffard. "Stay with Lady Joan until I return."

"No," she exclaimed. "Better he stays with you if there is danger. I'm not afraid for myself."

"My lady," Robbie said, "I swear there is no danger, and I have my own men with me." Indeed, Robbie had a full score of men-at-arms in his tail.

James nodded and patted her hand. "I've faced worse in France than any here will pose."

James remounted, with Robbie climbing back into the saddle beside him. William Wardlaw slapped his horse's withers to ride beside them, so they ended up with fifty men-at-arms in all riding behind them as Robbie put his horse into a trot and led them over a rise. "How bad?" James asked brusquely as they rode.

Robbie pressed his lips into a thin line that whitened with his tension. "Murdoch Stewart is furious at Atholl supporting your return. But the worst is Walter, his eldest son, a violent and rapacious man. He kidnapped the heiress of the earldom of Mar and forcibly married her. Does whatever he pleases and snaps his fingers even in his own father's face. But you'll judge for yourself."

James saw the first cot, a little thatch-roofed dwelling surrounded by a trampled barley field and a dead dog before the door. At least the place had not been torched. Robbie rode ahead, shouting a halloo, but got no answer.

"Dead? Or hiding?" James said. He had seen too many similar scenes in war-torn France. But Scotland wasn't war torn and such shouldn't be before him. "Robbie, with me." He drew his sword and kicked the door open. There were pots and bedding thrown about but no food and no sign of people. "Fled, then," he said with a sigh of relief. At least there were no corpses about.

They rode through another field, barley that was half trampled. There were no people tending it. All was silence. Then on the breeze James smelt smoke, not fresh but the ash of fires gone cold. Finally the remains of a village came into sight. James pulled his horse up to a slow walk, hand on his hilt as he rode toward the reeking debris, for there was nothing more than scattered heaps of charcoal where once there must have been cottages. There was more left of the church, for the walls still stood though the roof had fallen in. But there was no sign of people. A dog growled at the edge of a field of grain beyond the ruins as they rode closer. When James saw a body, shapeless and swollen, with its head hidden by a black swarm of flies, he sucked in his breath.

"You've seen this already," he said to Robbie.

"I rode through it on my way to greet you. The ones who did it had already gone. But they might have returned. Or some of the villagers might be hiding."

James nodded. "You're sure it was my cousin?"

Robbie shrugged. "No. Not certain."

"Why would someone attack this little place?" He

gestured around the hamlet. "There is nae even a lord's tower."

"It is a dispute over the benefice of yon church there," said Bishop William. "I'd heard of it but not of...this. Douglas claims it, but it was given to one of the Keiths."

"So why would Walter Stewart involve himself?" James swung from the saddle and turned in a slow circle, making a face as even his mouth filled with the taste of ash. The others hastily dismounted so as not to remain ahorse in the presence of the king.

"He fancies himself ruler of Scotland. He told his own father so, even struck him, it's rumored. Forbye Douglas is his friend. A boon companion. He took it as personal insult that his friend was slighted in the appointment."

A whimpery sound came from where the ravens had been. Tightening his stomach against what they might find, James tossed Iain his reins and went ahead on foot, the others trailing reluctantly after. When he pushed aside the stalks of barley, a woman crouched beside a body, rocking back and forth, her hands stuffed in her mouth, and a girl no more than two clung to her skirt. Another whimper, like the squeaking of a mouse, rose from the child.

James squatted and held his hands up, bare palms outward. "We'll do you no harm."

The woman stared at him, white showing all around her eyes. She made a sound that might have been a moan or a word. James couldn't tell.

"I'll see you have help, you and the lass," he said lowering his voice to nearly a whisper. He almost said they would see the bodies buried, but feared that would frighten her even more. "I swear it. On the Holy Rood." Blood had dried crusted on the woman's face. He couldn't tell how badly she was hurt. Could she even speak? "Is the lass hurt?"

This brought a response, and she hauled the whimpering

girl against her, finally uncovering her mouth. It was swollen, her teeth shattered from a blow.

"I'll see that no one hurts her." He sank lower onto his knees so he wouldn't seem threatening. "What's her name?"

"Anny," the woman lisped through her ravaged mouth and she pressed her cheek against the child's head, rocking. "She's Anny."

"I'll see you somewhere safe." He kept his voice carefully soft. "I give you my oath, but I need to ken who did this."

She shook her head and wailed, "I don't ken! There were men in armor. I don't ken who they were."

"Did they fly a banner? Was a lord with them?"

"I dinnae see a lord, but there was a banner. It was yellow with checkers in blue and white across it and the king's..." She grasped the child against her so hard that the whimpers grew into a faint wail. "The king's lion like on yours!"

James closed his mouth on a curse. Damn them. He'd been told that Murdoch and his son had combined the royal lion onto their own checky banners. Abruptly rising to his feet, he turned to Bishop William. "Have a cleric see they are cared for in God's mercy!" He whirled and stomped to his horse. Remounted, he clutched his reins so hard his horse snorted and stamped and the leather cut into his palms. He turned his horse's head and clapped his heels to its flanks, his teeth clenched in fury.

Chapter Seven

❦

Beams of light flowed over the interior of Melrose Abbey through its arched windows. Its golden walls gleamed as the light bounced off golden candlesticks and polished wood of the altar and rails. It took James' breath away standing here. Joan stood at his side wearing a gown of sea green trimmed with French lace like foam. Robbie Lauder was stationed at James' right, all clad in steel plate and a sword hanging from his belt. Men-at-arms in steel with pikes at their sides lined the long sides of the church, two hundred strong. The throng of bishops and lords in the cavalcade were shifting and looking nervous in clusters about the chamber.

James nodded to the herald to admit the two men who awaited outwith the doors. When the doors were thrown open, the herald intoned, "Regent of the realm and Duke of Albany, Murdoch Stewart and Lord Walter Stewart." Behind them, the aisle bristled with blades as the way was barred for entry to the regent's own men.

The first man through the doors storming toward him was a stranger but had the look of family in his large eyes and the bold lines of his face. The huge man who followed him seemed almost a stranger as well until he glared at James and growled, "Cousin."

Fifteen years past when he had last seen Murdoch Stewart, now Duke of Albany and Earl of Fife, in the Tower of London, he had been a strongly muscled man, though even then he had most often smelled of wine and had eyes blurred red with drinking. Now a coarse beard more gray than black covered his chin but not the sag of his jowls. Nothing could hide the bulk of his belly or the heavy bags under his eyes. His nose was stippled with the red of broken veins.

James lifted his chin. "I'll speak with you shortly, cousin," he said. "First, there is the matter of your son."

"You have more sense than I took you to have," Walter Stewart said as he strode up the long aisle of the church. "It is I you must speak to, for it is I who rule in Scotland. Not my father and most definitely not you." He thrust his fists onto his hips. "If you think my men outwith the Abbey will acknowledge your rule any more than I, you are wrong."

"I have seen the fruit of your rule, Lord Walter. Savage burning, rapine, and murder. Now it is time that you paid the price of that fruit. Robert Lauder, I command that you seize this man."

"Men! To me!" Walter Stewart whirled to run for the door. "Murder! Murder! To me!"

With a rasp of steel, Robbie Lauder drew his sword. The door burst open. Douglas shouted a command and his men dropped their pikes to form a hedge that blocked the way through the doors. Walter Stewart stood open mouthed, his sword half drawn, as Robbie approached him and shoved the point of his sword under his chin.

James let out a breath he hadn't realized he was holding. "There will be no bloodshed in the Abbey!" he commanded. "Walter Stewart, you are hereby confined to Lord Robert's castle of Bass Rock until it is my pleasure to try you before peers of the realm."

One of the men-at-arms grabbed the prisoner's sword from behind. The horrid tension left the room. James heard Joan's soft sigh. Robbie gave him a look. Yes, there was a deliberate irony in his choice, James acknowledged with a nod and a twitch of his lip.

"Take him out of my sight."

Murdoch Stewart watched his son being hauled, cursing, toward the door of a side chapel. Murdoch's mouth worked, opening and closing, but no sound came; then he turned to James and roared his anger. "Damn you, you puling pup! How dare you lay hands on my son?"

James raised an eyebrow. "I would nae soil my hands by touching him, Murdoch."

Murdoch staggered slightly as he took a step forward. "Soil your hands? Soil them? With the rightful ruler of this realm." He swayed and his anger seemed to let go. "I never could control the lad. Thrawn as my father and told me to my face that he would rule. Even threatened to take the great seal away from me."

"He will not." James looked at Murdoch and slowly shook his head. "Nor will you."

"Bloody hell, rule the damn kingdom and much joy to you. The nobles will fight you every step of the way. It was you or Walter would have it, any road." He pulled the seal, as big as the palm of his hand, from the purse at his belt and threw it onto the floor.

For a moment, James was so angry he could not speak. He strode to thrust his face into Murdoch's, flooding with heat. "I will see you at Scone Abbey when you place me on the throne," James said in an icy voice. "Until then, stay out of my sight. Get out."

Murdoch glowered at him through bleary, red-rimmed

eyes before he lurched through the door that a man-at-arms opened for him.

Iain Alway knelt to pick the Great Seal of Scotland up from the floor and thrust it into James' hands. James ran his fingers over the silver disk with its raised figure of a mounted knight. In some ways, this would be as much a symbol of his reign as a crown, its impression adorning every document he signed. "I will not use this until I am crowned, and Bishop William Lauder will be my Keeper of the Seal as well as chancellor," he said with a smile.

Chapter Eight

May 2, 1424

A deafening clamor of trumpets announced James' arrival. The May sunshine was warm on his bare head. He nodded to a man-at-arms, who threw open the doors of Scone Abbey before him. His heart pounded in his chest like the hooves of a racing steed. He clenched his fists at his sides to keep them from shaking. There was another blare of trumpets and he stepped through the doors and gave Murdoch Stewart an icy glare. As Earl of Fife, it was Murdoch's duty to place James on the throne. At least the man appeared to be sober, though the look he gave James scorched with fury.

Murdoch jerked his head toward the front of the abbey and stomped in that direction as James followed. The dozen trumpets made a cacophony that echoed from the stone walls as the crowd of nobles parted before them. James nodded to the right and left as he passed the host of bowing barons and lords and ladies, knights, magistrates, and provosts, and he couldn't keep a smile of satisfaction from curving his lips. Every noble in the kingdom was here, or near enough, though some had been sent to England to serve as hostages for his ransom. Lord Graham was there with James' elder sister, Mary, whom James barely remembered. The sharp-faced Isabella, Duchess of Albany, looked grim, standing beside a young man so fat James wondered if any horse would carry him. Robert Lauder bowed deeply amidst the crowd. A grin nearly split William Giffart's face. John Scrymgeour, the standard-bearer of Scotland, stood ready with the banner for his part in the ceremony, blank faced. James' last living uncle, the Earl of Atholl, watching with hooded eyes, met James' gaze. Whether they all were truly expressing a desire for his crowning or just curious didn't matter. Together with Bishops Lauder and Wardlaw, he had planned a coronation that would leave no doubt in their minds that James had claimed his throne.

It seemed to take an eon and less than a second for him to reach the gilded throne that sat beside the altar. James took his place. The rich smell of incense wafted through the air. Rainbow light flashed and shimmered from the huge windows, and a hundred candles set in gold candlesticks sent up prayers. *And I'm like to need every one of them.*

He nodded to the pudgy abbot, who bowed and went to a side door. When he led Joan in with her hand gracing his, the breath went right out of James' body. In ivory silk and French lace, she was even more exquisite than the first day he had seen her walking in a spring garden. The rainbow light awoke shimmers in the pearls that decorated the bodice of her dress. Her long, golden curls cascaded onto her shoulders.

Her eyes brimmed with tears when her gaze met his. Perhaps neither of them had truly believed that this day would come. He saw her throat work as the abbot seated her in a smaller throne on the opposite side of the marble altar. This the bishops had argued against for days. Queens were not crowned in Scotland, but James shouted them down. Joan would truly be his queen.

Bishop Wardlaw, in white vestments and red stole embroidered with gold and jewels, as Primate of Scotland, led out the other bishops, Bishop Lauder of Glasgow followed by the bishops of Moray, Argyll, Aberdeen, and Dunkeld, all in their greatest finery. They carried draped between them sumptuous purple and gold robes in which to drape him.

The trumpets silenced to an audible intake of breath from the crowd. James felt as though he might float; his limbs had no weight as he stood. The bishops decked him in the heavy robes that anchored his weightlessness to the ground. A sweet sound of boys chanting Glória in excélsis Deo in clear, high voices filled the air.

An acolyte handed Bishop Wardlaw a glass ampulla. He bowed, praying at the altar to consecrate it, before he carried it to stand before James. James tried to contain the rush of excitement as his pulse thundered in his ears. He sank to his knees and the bishop anointed him with oil, forming a cross on his forehead. He felt almost faint with the significance of the moment that made him truly a king.

Cymbals crashed and James flinched, looked up blinking. They crashed again and again. Bishop Wardlaw motioned to Murdoch, whose face purpled. He ground his teeth in fury when Wardlaw handed him the gold, jewel-encrusted crown. Pushing it onto James' head, he made a sound in his throat like a growl, but James did not care as shouts filled the abbey. "God save the king! God save the king! God save the king!"

The shouts and tumult drowned out even the clashing of cymbals that were joined by blaring of the trumpets. Looking across at Joan, he saw that tears were dripping down her cheeks. He would have gone to her to take her in his arms if he could have.

At last Bishop Wardlaw held up his hands and silenced the tumult. The cymbals stopped and, to the blast of the trumpets, the bishop brought James the scepter for his right hand. James' uncle, the Earl of Atholl, strode through the crush to kneel and hold out in both hands the sword of state. James laid his hand on it. Atholl whispered, "Welcome home, Your Grace," before he rose and took his place behind the throne as Scrymgeour accepted the huge Lion Rampart banner from a man-at-arms and took his place beside the earl.

The was a rustle through the crowd as though they expected the ceremony to end, but again Bishop Wardlaw held up both hands to silence them. There was a long pause. He turned to Joan, and she rose from the throne to sink onto her knees. He accepted a golden coronet from the Bishop of Moray and placed it over her honey-colored hair. Then he took her hands and led her to James.

James' heart thudded so hard he thought it might beat its way out of his chest as she knelt. She put both hands between his. In a voice soft and clear, she was the first to give him her oath of fealty.

Chapter Nine

James waved away the goblet of wine that a servant offered on a platter and growled his impatience at the new squire who was trying to buckle him into his armor. "Your Grace," he said in a voice that shook, "I cannot tell where this strap fastens."

"Damnation!" James swore. "Where is Iain? Go find him, and hurry." The lad flinched as Iain Alway said, "I am here, Sire. You're frightening him. No wonder he's all thumbs."

James hadn't seen Iain standing behind him in the door of the pavilion of Bishop Lauder.

James looked at the clumsy boy, Sanderis he was called, and one of the Douglases, taken on to please Wigtoun. Like all of the Black Douglases, he was plain of face, for they'd never been called a handsome family, and dark haired like the lot of them. He had a wisp of a moustache and eyes of obsidian. James sighed. Shouting wouldn't teach the lad what he needed to know. "Let Iain do it and you watch," he said. "You'll learn soon enough."

Iain nudged Sanderis out of the way and knelt to thread the strap into place. "One of the Douglases?" Lauder asked.

"Aye, though who had the teaching of him I dinnae ken. It couldn't have been Wigtoun, albeit was at his behest I took him on." He snorted a brief laugh. "A nephew or cousin. I cannae recall. The Douglases seem to have bred like rabbits. Who can keep them straight?"

"The Stewarts are as bad." Lauder smiled, but it quickly faded. "The talk is that you plan to ride in the jousting."

"I intend to do exactly that."

Bishop Lauder shook his head. "You have no business risking yourself in a joust. And what kind of dignity does that show when you allow a subject to trade blows with you? You're the king. Crowned. And they dinnae ken you. They need to see your kingly dignity—"

"I ken what they need to see!" James strode across the pavilion, whirled, and strode back. "They need to see a strong man who can stand up to a blow. They need a king who isn't afraid to face a foe. They need to see a king who...a king who is nothing like his father. To hell with sitting whilst other men fight, Lauder. They need to see that I am in the mold of the great Bruce, and I intend to show them so."

"Your Grace," the bishop said and patted a palm toward James as though to calm him, "it cannot be seemly for a subject to strike you. It would be lèse-majesté."

"Nonsense. Not in a joust. King Henry jousted often enough."

"Be sure my gorget is fastened aright, Iain," James said, but his gaze was fixed on the bishop. "Now get out." Bishop Lauder turned to leave, but James let out a gusty breath. He couldn't afford to quarrel with his few friends, and the bishop meant well. A churchman wouldn't understand these things like a fighting man. He called out, "Wait."

When the bishop turned back, James said, "You must believe that I ken what is best. Now have a cup with me before I ride." He motioned to the servant and took a cup as the bishop did as well. He took a drink. The wine was acid on the tongue, too long in the cask. He'd have to see about better wine being brought to the kingdom. He sat down, armor clanking. "It's a pity that Robbie isn't riding in the joust. I would have liked to try my skill against him."

"He prefers the melee. The mace is his weapon. He loves a close fight, it would seem."

"I should have commanded him, I suppose. Ah well, another time." He drained his cup and wiped his mouth on the back of his hand. "I rode against Harry Monmouth, did you ken? Even unseated him once, though like Robbie I'm better in the melee and better still at wrestling."

"Then why joust?"

"Because they'll all see me. In the melee I'd be lost in the crowd, one of many. Showing them who I am and that they can respect me is more important than what I love best. Too many think me a beggar king, a lapdog of the English. I must give that the lie."

Iain held out James' cloth-of-gold surcoat with his Lion Rampant picked out in gems on the chest. James stood and let Iain settle it over his head, then knelt to buckle his sword belt around his waist. "My people dinnae ken me, but after today, they will."

Bishop Lauder walked beside James, with Iain and Sanderis trailing, toward the jousting field. The grassy haugh of the River Tay spread out before them. It was abuzz with brightly dressed nobles, and commons in hodden-grey strolled toward hastily erected stands, horses were led as they snorted and tossed their manes, servants dashed through the crowd on errands. Chunks of meat sizzled over braziers, giving off a savory scent. Hawkers cried that they had meat pies and bread fresh from the oven. A herdsman leading a goat dropped to a knee as they passed. "My lords," he said as the goat butted him in the back and sent him onto his face. James laughed. He would have tossed the man a coin had he had one. His purse was still as empty as it had always been.

He watched Bishop Lauder take a place next to the queen. She had changed from her coronation finery, and her skin looked like rich cream against the blue silk. Her new crown gleamed against the braids in her golden hair, its sapphires a perfect match for her eyes.

James stood beside his horse, young Sanderis holding the reins, and Iain knelt to give him a boost into the saddle. In the heavy armor, mounting unassisted was possible but not pleasant, but James waited for the first rider to appear. He was to ride against the champion.

Alexander Stewart, youngest son of Murdoch, rode out on a fine-moving bay courser clad in gilded barding. Young Alexander glittered with gold from head to foot. Wigtoun entered the list in a blue surcoat with the crowned heart of the Douglases over steel armor that glinted in the sunlight. He got his gamboling horse in hand and took his position. He dropped his visor with a clang, ignoring the grinning Stewart, who bowed to the galleries. There were shouts and a few jeers as he set his lance.

James couldn't think the two men were well matched. Alexander was too much younger and inexperienced compared to Wigtoun, but he'd won the right in earlier jousts.

They both leaned forward and at the same moment kicked their horses into a fast canter. James held his breath as they closed in on each other. At the last second, Alexander tilted his shield. Wigtoun's lance scraped across it screaming, but the maneuver made the younger man miss with his own weapon. Wigtoun lurched in the saddle from the force he'd had behind his own blow.

There were a jeers and even a few laughs from the gallery.

Iain grunted and muttered, "Alexander doesn't have as much skill as he thinks he does."

James nodded as Wigtoun straightened in the saddle. Neither man had shattered his lance in the poorly done tilt, so they both trotted back into place. Young Alexander Stewart shouted something at a laughing spectator. There were more hoots and taunts. He spurred into a hard gallop, not even waiting for Wigtoun to start. James grunted. Wigtoun set his horse at a slower place, lance rock steady as he rode to meet his opponent. Half way up the tilt, he raked his horse with his spurs and leaned further forward, shifting his lance down. This time when Alexander tilted his shield, Wigtoun hit it in the low quarter so hard that he lifted the man out of the saddle before the lance shattered. Alexander's lance flew out of his hand and clattered at the base of the gallery. Alexander Stewart rolled in the grass.

James glanced to see that Joan was standing and clapping. The gallery had leapt as one to their its feet, shouting and cheering. Wigtoun raised his visor and bowed left and right to the cheers.

Alexander lurched to his knees. As his squire ran toward him, he jerked off his helm and flung it at the running lad, who didn't even have time to dodge. The force of the heavy helm in the belly knocked him on his arse, and the gallery broke into laughter again, whooping and shouting. Alexander stared around him, his face dark with fury. He stamped away, shouting at the squire as he went.

Wigtoun trotted up, his helm resting before him, and wiped sweat from his brow. "Aye. That went well." He shook his head laughing softly.

"And I'm going to knight him tomorrow..." James rested a foot on Iain's clasped hands and was given a lift as he flung himself into the saddle, reins in hand, he wheeled and grinned at Wigtoun. "Let's see if you find me a tougher opponent."

"Will I have your ire if I toss you on your arse as well?"

"You have to do it first."

James turned his horse's head and rode to his end of the cloth barrier that stretched between the paths of the two riders. He saluted the queen. His horse whickered and he said, "Steady, lad. Steady," quieting it with a touch. Iain handed him his lance. James couched it as Wigtoun took his place opposite.

James put his spurs to his horse's flanks, and it ran. Wigtoun's lance was steady as a bounder as they galloped at each other. The man was no trickster, but obviously he liked to use his bulk to defeat his opponent. James had to defeat him cleanly, clearly. So he gripped his lance harder and leaned farther over his horse's withers. He tightened his arm in his shield.

The two lances exploded in a shower of fragments. Pain shot through his shoulder from the force of the blow. His horse was on its haunches. He clasped the horse's flanks with his legs, half out of the saddle, grunted, and righted himself. When he could look up, Wigtoun was righting himself and cheers were going up from the gallery. He turned to look at Joan in the royal enclosure. She had jumped to her feet, hands pressed to her mouth. He tossed down the stump of his broken lance and gave her a brief wave.

Wigtoun took a fresh lance and laughed at something his squire said to him. James took his own with a nod of thanks. Wigtoun spurred at him at a hard gallop. James rode to meet him. Again the lances shattered and James felt as though his shoulder would shatter, but he managed not to reel in the saddle. Wigtoun threw down his broken lance in obvious disgust but gave James a courteous bow when they once more took their places.

Sweat dripped down James' face and the back of his neck.

The May afternoon wouldn't have been hot, but inside his armor was like an oven. Sweat dribbled down his sides.

Wigtoun took his time with settling his lance, so James thought perhaps he was tiring. Someone from the stands shouted for them to hurry it up, so he set his spurs to his horse and they thundered at each other again. The first times he'd used no technique, so he knew Wigtoun would expect the same again, but unlike Alexander, he had the strength to carry out a tricky hit. When Wigtoun's lance tip was an arm's length from his shield, James twisted in the saddle. It took all his strength to hold his own lance rock steady. Wigtoun had no time to adjust his aim and his lance scraped across James' golden shield with a lion rampant. James' hit solid. Wigtoun lifted straight backward from the saddle. He landed flat on his back with a clatter of armor, and the gallery burst into applause, cheers, whistles, and shouts. James smiled to see Joan clapping and Bishop Lauder beaming beside her.

James reined up at the end of the list. His lance hadn't even broken, and Iain ran out to take it from him. He paused until he saw Wigtoun's squire help him to his feet. The man directed a deep though somewhat wobbly bow in this direction before he walked off the field. Then James rode slowly past the gallery, waving, and dismounted to climb the steps to the royal gallery.

Joan shook her head at him. "What if you'd lost?" But she was beaming.

"Then they would have seen that the king expects honest fights."

As James walked Joan to the archery field along with Bishops Lauder and Wardlaw, Robert Lauder joined them along with a few others. "There are only a few archers," Robbie said. "It shan't compare to what you've seen in England, I'm afeart."

James frowned. "All men aren't required to practice with the bow?"

"Nae, each freeholder must provide his own kettle helm and leather gauntlets for when they are called. But only a few practice with a bow, mainly in the forest."

"I'll have to think on that. Since the Battle of Crécy, not having archers to call on is madness."

"Douglas has held his own in France with few archers," Wardlaw objected.

James hoped that Robbie was exaggerating the weakness in archers, but there were only twenty in the contest. That afternoon a lanky redhead named Adam Byset, a commoner from Lanark Forest, won the competition. He was good and easily outshot all the others. James added making a law that all men must practice at the butt to his long list of what he must accomplish. James sent Sanderis to seek him out to join James' train and had Bishop Lauder add a purse to sweeten the offer. Having to do so soured the moment for him, but not for long in the fragrant spring afternoon.

The mêlée that followed went on for an hour. Twenty-five men fought afoot, knights and squires, for the profit of ransom of anyone they defeated. James had forbidden the use of war axes as too dangerous, so they fought with tourney swords, and a few even used clubs. In a pandemonium of flying clods of dirt, sprays of blood, and swinging weapons, they rushed each other, first in small groups that then broke up to whale at each other. The defeated limped off the field, one with a shattered arm was carried, and two were dragged off, unconscious. The victor, Walter Haliburton, James' cousin through his mother, held his sword over his head and turned to the screams of the crowd. James chuckled at the reaction. His coronation and the celebration could hardly have been more successful.

That night at the banquet at Blackfriars Monastery in

Perth, James was happier than he had ever been in his life. The Earl of Atholl was grinning and drinking deep of the wine, Murdoch Stewart was nowhere to be seen, nor the two of his sons still not imprisoned, and Joan was beaming as they listened to minstrels. Wigtoun had taken his defeat with good grace and sat next to the king in high good humor.

"My shoulder will ache for a week," James said happily, rubbing where the muscles had taken the brunt of Wigtoun's blows.

"I was surprised that you took the chance," Wigtoun said. "I dinnae throw at the tilt."

James frowned. "I never thought that you did, nor wanted you to."

Joan leaned forward to speak past James. "King Henry jousted often enough and even lost on occasion." She shrugged. "It's not that I like His Grace taking chances, but I know the kind of king he means to be, so he must start as he means to go."

Later, while he wandered through the vast hall with Joan on his arm and watched the mirth and dancing, Bishop Lauder joined them. "Are you ready for tomorrow?" James asked.

Lauder ran his hand through his hair. "I am. But I do not ken what I can do to make it easy. It has been almost twenty years since the last parliament. People no longer look to it, and you plan such changes..." He stuttered and looked for a phrase. "...such changes that the nobles will not accept happily."

"As long as you're ready," James said. He hoped he had planned well enough to accomplish what he needed, but he knew depending on guile, as he must, was a risk. "I ken what I am doing."

Much later, he took Joan back to their chambers and their lovemaking sent her to sleep, her hair spread out. He ran his hand down his sweat-slicked chest and went to the window to open the shutters and let in the sweet night air. He noticed the glow of a candle from a window though the night was half gone, and two of the last of the revelers stumbled across the yard, holding each other up.

James remembered the few times he had attended the English parliament. They had not been friendly to King Henry's demand for more gold and men for his war, but Henry had prevailed in the end. Pray God and the saints he had learned enough from that strange, hostile mentor to prevail as well.

Chapter Ten

Through the high, narrow windows of the Blackfriars' cavernous refectory, where just the night before they had reveled, morning sunlight spilled, laying golden stripes across the granite floor. The stone walls were bare as befit a religious house. James sat on one side of the dais in the Abbot's high-backed chair of gleaming oak. On the opposite side, Bishop Lauder took his place as chancellor, whose duty it was to preside over what James had every expectation would be a raucous gathering. The Earl of Erroll, Lord High Constable of Scotland, took a place behind James and Lord Scrymgeour, the banner-bearer of Scotland, in the rear.

He could feel the unease in the air as lords and knights as well as prelates and burghers took their places. The chatter was low and uneasy. All three estates had been commanded under the severest of penalties to attend. After his taking prisoner of Walter Stewart, apparently they had not wanted to test him, not yet anyway. He moved slightly in the chair with its thin cushion, sure his arse would soon be numb. But at least he had a cushion. The parliament was consigned to long, hard oak benches normally used for monks at their meals.

When the benches were at last filled, Bishop Lauder rapped a gavel. When silence didn't fall, he rapped harder. "My lords temporal and spiritual, barons, lords, and burgers," he intoned in a voice that filled the vast room. "His Grace, King James, has a number of provisions which this first parliament of his reign shall consider and enact for the good and peace of the realm."

A blare of four trumpets announced the next part of the ceremony and a side door was thrown open. The first of the candidates swaggered in clothed in a white linen tunic: Alexander Stewart, Murdoch's youngest son. Dark haired like his father in his youth, but clear eyed and muscled, he looked more of a knight than his father ever had, but he made no attempt to hide his pride and arrogance. James wondered if this was a mistake, but perhaps knighting him would help bring at least some of that ilk to side with the crown. Alexander continued his way to kneel in front of the dais and the rest followed: Walter Giffard, whom he owed so much, Seton of Gordon, young Robert Graham, Douglas, Earl of Wigtoun, Lord Lyon, and Walter Haliburton, the son of Sir Walter Haliburton, who had helped James escape to Bass Rock all those years ago. The earls of Angus and Mar followed, for knighthoods had been long neglected with no king to perform them.

James' heart thudded, and he realized this was the first ceremonial occasion of his reign. None of them would ever forget this. He held out his hand to the Lord High Constable, who handed him the sword of state. James stepped first to Walter Giffard. Alexander gave a smothered grunt, but James tapped his faithful squire on each shoulder, a gentle blow that King Henry had served him those years ago. "Avance, Chevalier, au nom de Dieu," he pronounced. Walter grinned up at him and arose. James moved on to Alexander Stewart and then to the next. By then his heartbeat had slowed. But he still felt a flush of excitement to be finally acting as king.

When the last of the new knights took their places on the benches, for all were part of the parliament, James sat. He nodded his permission at Bishop Lauder, who cleared his throat. They had consulted long over the order in which the new laws should be presented. James was not sure that any would be less difficult than another.

Lauder began with those least likely to cause an uproar. "The king proposes that there will be weekly musters of men for training in arms and archery for all men between the ages of sixteen and sixty," he announced. "The parliament will impose export duties on cattle, horses and hides shipped from all Scottish ports. Warfare and disturbing of the king's peace or failure to aid the king in maintenance of that peace shall be deemed treason, and the lands of any so acting shall be forfeit. Further to that peace, no one shall take to the road with an excess of retinue in arms to be limited to a score for an earl, twelve for a bishop or lord, eight for a knight or abbot, and six for a prior or gentleman. That in the furtherance of trade, hostelries shall be built in all towns of the realm with stables, chambers and with bread and ale and fodder at reasonable prices." He droned on for several minutes and James watched as the tension eased out of the room. Some were nodding; no one seemed surprised or bothered by the acts so far as he had hoped.

The burghers were the least powerful of the estates and James had decided that putting an enactment that would anger them would probably soothe the lords when they found out exactly what he had planned. It would be a sour dose for the burghers to swallow but must be done. He nodded to the chancellor, who continued, "All burghers of this realm will collect from the burgesses, guilds, and citizens a portion of the king's ransom in the amount of ten thousand Scottish merks within the year."

The burghers, who were mostly in the back and around the edges of the refectory, were on their feet shouting, but James noticed a number of the noblemen nodding in satisfaction. Of course, they didn't mind seeing the heavy ransom paid by someone other than themselves. A burly, heavy-shouldered man in blue merchant's robes strode toward the dais, his face mottled red. "You will ruin us! We shouldn't have all the weight of the taxes!"

"There will be no disturbance in my presence." James gave the man an icy glare. "I will not permit lèse-majesté. So take your seat or you will find yourself in a dungeon." The High Constable took a threatening step forward, but the burgher quickly retreated, though not looking any less angry. James knew the man had been no threat, but establishing his authority early was essential.

The smirking nobles who did not object to new taxes falling mainly on others would soon be less pleased. James let the din go on for several minutes before he made a sign to Bishop Lauder to silence them.

When Bishop Lauder announced that all gold and silver mines were to be declared property of the Crown and no gold would be sent beyond the borders of the kingdom, the Bishop of Moray, Columba de Dunbar, a spare, white-haired man in a high-necked black cassock and massive gold pectoral cross on a gold chain, quickly stood. "You can nae mean to prevent payments of gold to be sent to the Papal Curia. That is...unthinkable."

Bishop Wardlaw stood and glared at the clerics until an uneasy silence fell on the room. "That is exactly what the king means. We can no longer impoverish the realm with an excessive flow of precious metals to the Roman curia. What is more, I have agreed with the King's Grace that no cleric is to leave or send a procurator over the sea without his express consent." He swept the room with a heavy gaze. "Is there any here who would dispute my right?"

Above a current of murmurs from both the nobility and the burghers, James said, "Then you, Reverence. Scotland needs its gold far more than His Holiness. I gave him my support whilst I was imprisoned, so I am sure he will not begrudge rebuilding my realm after its long years of neglect."

The cleric was shaking his white head, his mouth open as though to continue the argument, but James motioned to Bishop Lauder to continue.

"Any feudal holder of lands shall produce his charter thereof before the king's Sheriffs to prove right of possession—"

A hubbub of shouts drowned his words out. Every noble in the hall was on his feet, some shouting, and others turned to a neighbor, hands and arms working as they gesticulated and exclaimed, but James noted that the burgher in blue was chuckling. Bishop Dunbar crossed his arms and looked thoughtful while the other clergy nodded and exchanged whispers. James looked at Bishop Lauder. The uproar was unseemly for the greatest in the land, but James knew they needed to express their outrage before he had them reined in. When James finally nodded, the bishop hammered with his gavel and bellowed for silence. Even when Lauder pounded with his gavel and used his impressive voice yelling for silence, it took several minutes for order to be restored. "There shall be a levee of one shilling in each merk of land value on all landowners whatsoever, toward payment of the king's ransom in order that the hostages now held in England maybe returned."

The nobles looked at each other, some glaring, others not meeting their neighbor's gaze. Nearly every noble family likely to object had a son or brother now a hostage. James had seen to it. He stood, his head beginning to throb from the tension. The four trumpets sounded an ear-shattering blast, and the silence was thunderous as the men stared open mouthed. "The morn we will discuss these proposals and the following day vote upon them. And I shall have good order or shall have the High Constable and his men enforce it. Do I make myself clear?" He strode from the refectory with his chancellor on his heels.

In his chamber, he scrubbed his face with his hands, and Lauder let out a gusty breath.

"How did it go?" Joan asked.

James would have liked her to have been able to hear the proceedings, but there was no gallery where she could have listened. He motioned for Sanderis to pour him a mug of ale. "Leave us," he told the lad and took a deep drink. The ale was dark and thick and strong enough that his eyes stung, but it began to ease the thudding in his forehead. When the door was closed, he sank into a chair next to the hearth. "I thought not ill. None were happy, but there will be enough divisions that I can turn each to my advantage."

"As we discussed," Lauder said, nodding. "But it will nae be easy, Your Grace."

James barked a brief laugh. "The nobles will fight hardest against proving their estates. Too many of them received estates they had no right to. I mean to have back those that Albany gave up without right. And the taxes are a bitter potion, but if they have any hope of return of the hostages, then they'll agree to them."

Lauder coughed. "Not that you intend for all to return..."

"I don't understand," Joan said as she sat. "Not all?"

This was a part of his plan he had yet to share with her. She might not approve, but he knew she would come to agree when he explained the value of seeing that least some of their enemies being outwith the kingdom. But with his head still throbbing and a long day of wrangling on the morrow, he didn't want to argue, so he said, "So large a ransom to pay, many will be a long time in returning."

She gave him a narrow-eyed look, but the bishop offered her a cup of malmsey and asked James if he thought the Earl of Atholl would support him in the vote, so the subject was dropped.

Chapter Eleven

August 1424

The jennets pulling the litter were led by their horse master on a well-made gelding. He, like the rest of their escort of fifty men, wore the king's livery with the Lion Rampant. The riverside road cut its way along the gorse- and bracken-covered braeside of Gilmerton down on Edinburgh. James saw the shape of Edinburgh rising before them, dyed gold in the afternoon sun.

James called for a halt and stepped down from his mount. Joan pushed back the curtain. Before he could offer her his hand, she leapt out in a flurry of silken skirts. James caught her arm in his hand with an anxious, "Be careful, love."

She laughed at him. "I'm not so far gone, Your Grace, that I cannot descend from a stuffy litter." She gave a tiny shrug. "And I needed the fresh air."

"Are you feeling ill?" He couldn't help that he was anxious even though she laughed at him. She was five months gone, and he had no experience of women with child. "Are you sure you feel well enough to ride a horse into the city?"

But Joan was staring at the city in the distance with a

smile of delight brightening her face. "Could we not visit more often? It is amazing." Within the narrow confines of the walls, every building heaved several stories upward into a crazy skyline of tall steeples, gables, and towers surrounding narrow streets. From the green of the surrounding plain and the blue of the Firth of Forth to the north, it thrust upward before them like a mailed fist. The capital city of the realm was built on a constricting ridge so that the walled city was scarcely a mile long and only half that in width, and the height of Castle Rock glowered down Edinburgh Castle over all.

"Aye, if you like, of course." He was much minded to give her anything she wanted, though this visit was purely business to oversee his nobles presenting the charters to their land. Few of his laws had caused so much resistance and anger. "Bring Her Grace's horse."

The gates were opened, awaiting them, when they reached them, and the church bells sounded. The Provost met them with bows and a greeting in his broken Latin to escort them into the city. The streets were jammed with crowds shouting greetings to their brawny king and his satisfactorily expectant queen, whilst amongst them bakers' boys shouted, "Hot pies!" and on one of the corners a Franciscan mendicant in gray robes and a rope belt was praying loudly.

Joan, as always, was untroubled by riding even with her belly visibly swelled with their first child. He should have known he was worrying for nothing, James thought, as she smiled and waved. She was healthy and blooming as a primrose in spring. Beginning to relax now he felt sure she was untroubled, James did the same, but when he looked up at the dark castle that was their destination, he scowled. He would never love staying in this place nor any other castle. They would always remind him too much of a prison. No, as soon as might be, he would have builders at Linlithgow, which had been much neglected of late and in need of repairs, but the lochside palace would be a fine place to show his people what a king's court should be.

"They are coming to love you," Joan said as they rode through the wide space of the Grassmarket that was now packed with people. Their outriders had to clear a way through the press with shouts of "Make way for the king!" pushing people back with the weight of their horses. Soon their horses' hooves rang on the cobbled street up the steep hill to the east side of the castle.

The gates to Edinburgh Castle were open and the guards armed with pikes lowered their points and stepped aside when James and his Queen came trotting up.

An hour or so later, after Joan admitted she was weary from the journey, James escorted her to their chamber. Tired and dusty from the journey though he was, he said the business of state was too important to wait and sent word to his chancellor and his new secretary, John Cameron, to meet him in the council chamber. He turned from the door, and the sunlight caught in her hair like a nimbus. "Joan?"

"What?"

He held out his hand. "Kiss me first."

The council chamber was sparsely furnished, the floor covered in rushes and the walls hung with threadbare banners, with a rather plain council table in the center.

James took the chair at the head of the table, a Lion Rampant embroidered on the lumpy cushion, when Bishop Lawler came in, looking even more drawn than usual from their long journey and followed by John Cameron, a youngish cleric with dark hair clipped short around his tonsure and a beak of a nose, his arms full of papers.

"Your Grace," the chancellor said, "forgive the delay, but I kent you would want the lists of those who had proven their claims and even more importantly those who have..." He cleared his throat. "...those who have refused."

"How refused?"

"They have not appeared with their charters and turned away my men from their castles. Others are still slow to respond, but only two have defied your commands."

"Who?" James said with a chill in his voice.

"The Earl of Lennox and Sir Robert Graham. Others who are, I think, waiting to see the outcome number a score."

James was stunned. "A full score forbye to those two?"

"Many hold alienated crown lands that Murdoch or his father sold or gave away to curry favor. Others are simply stubbornly resisting like a horse too long left without a rider."

"And if I allow those two to defy me, the rest will follow."

"Graham is easily enough dealt with," John Cameron said mildly. "But Lennox is another matter, as Your Grace must see. He's an old man, stubbornly holding to power to which he's accustomed, and Murdoch's goodfather, Buchan—Murdoch's brother. He has at least four thousand men at his back in France, and the Douglas would doubtless side with Buchan and Murdoch. They may be in France, but their army has to be considered."

"And yet Wigtoun has consistently sided with me."

"Would he if Douglas, his own father, attacked you?" Bishop Lauder asked. "Though returning from France with their army would not be an easy or quick matter. Yet I fear they would feel they had to support Lennox if you act against him. Already there are rumors that Buchan will return to raise additional men."

"Which I cannae allow," James said, perhaps too sharply from the look the two men gave him. He should remember that both were on his side, so he said in a softer tone, "I'm weary from the journey. I must think. We will resume the morn, and I'll hear your advice then."

He stood, nodded to the two men who scrambled to their feet, and made for the door. Cameron opened it for him. He was walking toward the stairs when a guard came hurrying in from the bailey yard followed by a filthy man-at-arms with unkempt beard and in battered armor.

"Your... Your Grace," the guard stuttered. "He says he is messenger from France."

The man bowed awkwardly to James, who rubbed his forehead wearily with a sigh before he asked the man's name.

"Patrik, My Lord, of Dalkeith."

"Your Grace, man. You're speaking to the King of Scots," the guard snapped.

The man grimaced. "I was supposed to give the news to Wigtoun, the earl's son." He glared first at the guard and then at James. "But I suppose I might tell him first."

"How dare you?" The guard lowered his pike but paused at a gesture from James, and another stepped threateningly toward the messenger.

"Of course Wigtoun must have any news of his father." James softened his words with a slight smile. "Aye, and I'll see you rewarded for bringing it. What news is this, then?"

"There was a battle at a place called Verneuil."

James nodded. "I ken the place you mean."

"We took the town. I dinnae ken why the French charged when they did. But the Duke of Bedford cut them to pieces. The French broke. Routed. That left us surrounded. It was a slaughter. They were out for revenge, and they had it. We made a stand but...the whole Scottish army. The Earl of Douglas with them. The Earl of Buchan. Sir Walter Lindsay. I dinnae ken who escaped, but I was left for dead on the field. There was nothing to do but bring back the news to Wigtoun." The man shook his head. "Nae, he's the Earl of Douglas now."

James took a deep breath and said not a word. His chancellor and secretary and the guards had fallen quiet as the man told his tale. The only sound came from the shout of a sergeant out in the bailey yard. James thought of his own battles in France, the many times the English had done the same when he was with them. It could have been him killing his own subjects. But it hadn't been and this changed—much.

"Buchan and Douglas both dead then," James whispered. "You're sure of it? They weren't taken prisoner?"

"I saw them fall in the last charge."

"God have mercy on their souls," the chancellor said.

"Aye," James responded absently, and then shook himself from his reverie. "See that Patrik is given a bed and a warm meal." He turned to Cameron. "We must send word to Wigtoun at once by the fastest courier possible. And send for William de Hay, the High Constable. There are two men in the realm whom he must bring into custody."

"Into custody? You mean—"

James cut his secretary off. "The two are to be held in the strong castles, there to await trial. At my pleasure. Let others learn from it for the nonce. And whilst I decide what they will forfeit for their defiance." James strode for the stairs.

Chapter Twelve
DECEMBER 25, 1424

Joan awoke, the chamber cloaked in shadows. She tried to raise herself on one elbow but fell back with a moan. Her lips were so dry that when she moaned, she felt them crack. At once, James was beside her, kneeling on the edge of the bed, softly stroking her hair back from her forehead.

"What do you need, love?"

"Thirsty," she croaked.

He lifted her with an arm behind her shoulders and held a cup to her lips and she sipped. The watered wine felt wonderful as it slipped down her throat. She ached all over. No one had ever told her how much birthing hurt. She felt tears prickle her eyelids. "I wanted you so much," she whispered. "I begged them to let you come to me even though I knew it wasn't fitting. I'm ashamed."

He breathed a soft laugh. "I would have come if they'd have let me. I fought in France, have seen things I'll never speak of, far worse things than a bonnie lass being born."

"Where is she? I saw her...but it's all so fuzzy in my mind." She tried to push herself higher to see where her baby was, a feeling of panic going through her like a spark. "Where is my daughter?"

"Whist, love. She's well." But Joan clutched his arm, her eyes burning with tears. Perhaps he was only soothing her and there was something wrong with the child. Newborn babes often died. He motioned and the wet nurse approached the bed. James took the sleeping lass and laid her in Joan's arms.

She kissed the top of the babe's head, her hair reddish-brown fuzz as soft as silk. She had never felt what was in her breast now, a tenderness that was overwhelming. "She's beautiful. Isn't she beautiful?"

James chuckled and Joan looked up at him suspiciously. Was he laughing at their beautiful girl? But he reached a finger to stroke the wrinkled little hand and tiny fingers curved around it. "Of course, she is bonnie. She's your daughter."

Joan's stomach made a nervous jump when she remembered that she wasn't supposed to be happy for having a daughter. "I was afraid you were disappointed that it's not a son."

"In a bonnie lass? Nae, love." He settled her back on her pillows and kissed the corner of her mouth.

"She seems strong and sturdy." The fear returned. Newborn babies died so often, even ones that seemed strong sometimes. They mustn't wait a moment longer than necessary to be sure that she was under God's protection. "Bishop William will do the christening, will he not, James? Tomorrow?"

"Aye, on the morn, Love." He stroked her hair back again. "The Douglas godfather and his lady wife as godmother. I'll tell you about it after it's done. You have my word."

Joan kissed the baby's forehead. "We haven't chosen a name. Have you thought of one? We must do that before she's christened."

"I thought if you like we could call her for your mother. Margaret."

Joan felt tears prickle her eyes. She tried not to let James know how much she missed home and her mother. She was trying so hard to feel that Scotland was home, but often it seemed so strange and foreign, and sometimes they looked at her with such suspicion in their eyes. "You'd do that for me?"

He smiled. "We might not mention that it's for your mother. Everyone will think it is for St. Margaret. But you'll ken, and that is all that matters."

She managed a smile though her lips trembled. "It can be for both, can it not? St. Margaret was a queen the English sent to the Scots, so...it seems right somehow that she be named for both."

Chapter Thirteen

MARCH 1425

The main business of the parliament was over, and a long, boring business it had been, however necessary. Eight days of it to salvage the work of his first parliament, for too many of those laws had been ignored and flouted, so that he'd forced through a provision that his laws were to be kept and that any who broke them were to face severe punishment.

James knew he couldn't be too forward in clipping the wings of his out-of-control nobles, but he would see it done. There were other matters: he had thought John Cameron's idea of having a wise and loyal advocate for the poor who were taken before a judge was an excellent idea, though no realm James had ever heard of had such a law. They had wrangled for hours over that, over penalties for stealers of greenwood and destroyers of dovecotes. They'd especially squabbled over his own revenue being increased by customs on woolen cloth and salmon exports, but he had fought them until he won the funds that would give them a royal court that could be kept in decency. Damned if he would live like a savage.

As before, James had saved the most contentious for last when he had to hope they were all to weary to fight him.

Bishop Wardlaw droned on about the inquisition of heresy and that all so charged should be punished under the law of the church. The throne was damnably hard in spite of a thin cushion, and James shifted because his arse had long since gone numb. He could almost understand why Albany had not held parliaments whilst he was regent. Sweat trickled down James' back in the moist heat of a May afternoon. He hitched at the sleeves of his red velvet doublet, adjusting them so the yellow silk lining showed.

James had no intention that the Church would run Scotland. Just as he was reining in the rule of the nobles, so he would that of the Church. He waited until a pause in Wardlaw's rant on punishing heretics to nod to Cameron, who stood and bowed respectfully to the primate. "Of course, all children of Mother Church know that such deception must be put an end to, Reverence. But in order to control the flow of preachers and others who might bring disorder to the realm, The King's Grace proposes that any churchman or his embassage proposing to enter or leave the realm must first gain permission of the crown. As well, all appointments to benefices within the realm must first receive approval of the crown." Cameron gave a tight, smug smile. "Thus, disorder may be prevented."

Half the clerics in the hall were on their feet shouting and waving their arms. The rest were whispering to one another. Wardlaw stared at James, pulling at his lower lip thoughtfully.

When Cameron's pounding with his gavel had quieted the hall, Wardlaw said, "Your Grace, His Holiness will take such laws as an attack on the Church. I beg you reconsider. Controlling the gold that leaves Scotland, the Pope understands, but this is an extreme measure. I'm afeart you risk excommunication."

"No attack on the Church is intended." James leaned forward and scanned the room, giving each cleric, one by one, a hard look. "I supported Pope Martin in his dispute and have been always a good Christian, but I am sworn to protect the realm of Scotland. I mean to do so. Too many clerics leave for the Holy See, only to work against the good of the realm there." He smiled and gave a sop to the bishop's feelings. "And some enter the realm to spread heresy. This I shall stop."

He couldn't control the parliament without aid of the Primate of Scotland, but if the Primate wanted power over heretics, he would give something up. But now the nobles and burghers were looking every bit as weary and restless as James felt. Everywhere men were squirmed on the hard benches as comfortably they could. Murdoch sat slumped with his head in his hands.

James frowned when a servant slipped in a side door to sidle up to the Earl of Atholl. The hard-faced earl jerked a parchment from the servant's hand, broke the seal with his thumb, and perused it, his lips thinning to a hard line. He rose to his feet and said, "Sire, I must interrupt. There is dire news."

"Can this not wait?" Wardlaw said. "Our business is not complete."

"No, Your Reverence, it cannae. Your pardon, but this is of the utmost urgency. Rebellion is brewing in the west with an army to be led by Lord Johne Stewart."

Murdoch jumped to his feet. "Lies!" He pointed at the earl, his hand visibly shaking. "You...traitorous deceiver!"

James could feel the tension in the room like the string of a harp tightened until it would snap. The lords, burghers, and clerics all strained past each other to see the two men. James could not pretend to be totally surprised. At some point, his conflict with the other Stewarts had been bound to come to an explosion. His face pallid and damp with sweat, Bishop Lauder began to pound his gavel. "My lords," though his voice was thin, it dripped with scorn, "you are in the presence of the king. Another word and I'll have the guards enforce order."

Murdoch looked about him, his hands clasping and unclasping and face mottled red with fury.

James crooked a finger to the High Constable, William de Hay, a handsome man but for a nose flattened in a tourney, James had heard. "Have your men see the Duke of Albany to a chamber so that he can calm himself. I shall send for him."

"Fool!" Murdoch shouted. "He's a lying dog. He sided with my father, always. He's deceiving you." He was backing toward the door and fumbling as though looking for a sword, though there was no scabbard at his side in the parliament.

"May I have your permission to see to it myself?" Hay asked. "To prevent...conflict."

James nodded his consent. Hay bowed courteously to Murdoch and motioned for the man to precede him, although two guards stood ready with pikes in hand. After releasing a pent breath, Murdoch turned on his heel and stomped down the long path to the door of the refectory.

James had spent his entire life knowing that it would come to this moment, yet he was king and knew he must be seen to act within the laws he had made himself. "Now, uncle, what proof do you have of this uprising of my cousins, and who is involved?" he asked, trying to contain his fury. They had killed his brother, harried his poor father to his grave, and seen that he spent his entire life in an English dungeon. They deserved whatever punishment he gave them.

Atholl waved the message he had unsealed toward James. "I suspected something when no one kent where Murdoch's youngest pup, the fat one, Lord James, was, and I heard a rumor that Domhnall of Lennox was raising men. I sent one of my men to scout them out. Apparently they installed one of their own in Bass as a guard to take messages to Walter, so he is part of the plot. And whatever Murdoch says, he kent of it even though he's so drunken and fainthearted, he's agreed make Walter regent when you..." Atholl hesitated and then shrugged. "...when they'd disposed of you."

"Who else?" asked Bishop Wardlaw. "It can't be only young Lord Johne."

"They loosed Robert Graham, and he's joined them. Domhnall of Lennox is with them as well. Finlay, Bishop of Argyll, has declared Murdoch rightful king. Young Alexander is part of it, and Murdoch's secretary Alan of Otterburn has written a letter that went between them. Montgomery of Ardrossan has been their courier."

James heard muttering and nervous whispers throughout the refectory. The lords and burghers alike knew what that meant. The Bishop of Argyll being on the Albanys' side would allow them to raise a large army. James studied their faces. No wonder they were nervous; they had no reason to believe that James was strong enough to deal with an uprising, and they might pay with their lives or their lands for supporting him.

Alexander Stewart, Earl of Mar, was looking thoughtfully at Atholl, his elbows resting on his thighs and big hands hanging between his knees. Nearing fifty, he'd acquired the bulge of a solid belly under his silk doublet and was balding, with a close-cropped red beard that followed the line of his heavy jaw. He looked toward James and their gazes locked. Alexander was a bastard, and at least that meant that he had no designs on the throne.

"You have good information, my lord," Bishop Lauder said. "That was a most informative note that you read so quickly."

Atholl closed his mouth and studied the bishop, a

glimmer of light in his eyes. James wasn't sure if what he saw there was anger or approval. Atholl's mouth, framed by his busy moustache, was a thin slit and his face stony as a statue. He crossed his arms over his thick chest. "Aye, it told me much but not all. I do not ken where they mass their forces. Somewhere near Lennox is my guess. Nor do I ken when they plan to strike."

James was squeezing the arms of the throne so hard his fingers were stiff. He forced them loose and flexed them before he spoke. He felt as pale as Bishop Lauder looked, and his stomach was a stone in his belly. "How many kent of this? Of your certain knowledge. Murdoch? Who else?"

"Search his chambers for letters, nephew," Atholl said. "I am told that he has been corresponding with all three of his sons on this conspiracy, but I have not seen the letters to swear to. Have Walter's prison searched as well. That will tell you truth of the matter."

"Uncle, I thank you. I owe you a debt for your aid and it will be repaid. I propose to bestow upon you in life-rent the earldom of Streathern in gratitude." He stood and immediately all rose to their feet. "My lords of Douglas, Angus, and Mar, you shall attend me in the council chamber. Lord Lyon, close the doors of the abbey and see that none depart without my express command. Word of this must not leak out until we are ready to act."

He turned to Bishop Lauder. "Bring the Primate and my secretary to the council chamber as well." He bowed to Bishop Lauder, and the trumpets sounded as he stalked away.

James paced the room, firing himself up for what must be done and making decisions. When he realized his councilors couldn't sit, he motioned Bishop Lauder and Bishop Wardlaw to their places around the table. Neither was fit to stand, but he needed to move while he grappled in his mind with open rebellion. "John, send guards to search Murdoch's chambers."

"Would he be such a fool as to carry letters of treason with him?" his secretary wondered.

"He has always been a fool, and so my uncle thinks. Send word to Robbie Lauder to hold Walter Stewart under the heaviest guard with men he is sure of, forbye to make sure that he has no chance to destroy evidence. Search his room and his person for letters. Robbie must seize any letters they have managed to sneak in."

The new Earl of Douglas since his father's death in France and still earl of Wigtoun came in, followed by the Earl of Mar and the young Earl of Angus. At last James took his place at the head of the table. "We must act, and quickly, before they have time."

"It will take time to raise a host," Mar said. "It was at your command I came with merely a score men as your laws demand." He motioned to the others. "That is true of all of us."

James tapped his fingers on the table. "No, but we must see that they don't take us unawares. I'll send my cousin Sir Johne Stewart with as many men as we can spare to reinforce the garrison at Dumbarton, and from there he can send out scouts to locate the rebels. And we pull the asp's fangs in the east. I declare the parliament prorogued. Douglas, you are to hunt down Alexander." He slammed his fist down on the table. "Damn him, I knighted him with my own hand. Find all that my uncle named. I want them in irons within the hour."

Lauder gaped at him. "Parliament has never been prorogued in Scotland."

"I have no choice. It cannae continue to sit whilst there is open rebellion, but it must be ready to resume when these villains come to trial. Forty days to call a new parliament would be too long. The English have some ideas I mean to adopt, and this is one of them. Instead of calling a new parliament, we shall continue this one after a pause."

John Cameron rose to carry out James' command but paused at the door. "There is one name not mentioned that you might give thought to, Sire."

"Who might that be?"

"The Duchess Isabella. They say that it is she who rules that household. I dinnae know how true the rumors are, but..." He shrugged. "It is not something I would ignore. I cannae think that it was that slug Johne the Fat or his drunken father that came up with this scheme."

James gave a curt nod and the secretary quietly closed the door behind him. "Angus, I leave the Duchess to you. Take a sufficient force to seize Doune Castle where she bides if they resist. Arrest her and confine her to your own Tantallon Castle to hold her fast. If it was her mind that devised this scheme, I fear we'll find no proof of it, and my name would be stained beyond redeeming if she died. Treat her fairly—but no need to be over-gentle. A single maidservant and a cell with a bed and chamber pot shall suffice. She may have her sewing and attend chapel. And see that she comes to no harm."

He stood. "My lord of Mar, they say you are the best soldier in Scotland. I shall have a chance now to see if that is true. Raise as many men as you may with speed, and we'll lead them to Lennox."

Douglas had jumped to his feet with a scowl. "What of me?"

"They say the Douglas men are fine soldiers as well, so prove it to me."

Chapter Fourteen

James beat his hand on his armored thigh, a message crushed in it. The rebels had attacked Dumbarton, put it to the sword and flame, and his cousin Sir John with all his men died defending it. James was sure that for Dumbarton Castle on its high rock to have been entered, a traitor had opened the gates. It seemed that all within had been taken by surprise. In the morn, they'd ride for Dumbarton and pick up the trail of the rebels.

Their camp sprawled for two miles near the River Clyde. Standing in front of his pavilion, he looked out on a dozen more and a hundred cook fires. The men were wrapped in cloaks, giving out snores and grunts in their sleep whilst lightning bugs darted above them like sparks from the fires. Away in the distance he heard someone cursing. Further on, there was the snort and a brief whinny from the horses' pickets. Against the faint light of dawn that rimed the horizon, he saw a sentry marching his post.

Wisps of fog drifted off the river like trailing shrouds. A horn blared harooo and then another, the signal of the sentries for enemies approaching. Mar stepped out of his pavilion and shouted for his squire. "What direction is that?" he called. "Where is my damned squire?"

James shouted for Sanderis. A horn called again from the east, wild and urgent. Danger! Danger! Men were stumbling to their feet with shouts and questions, leather creaked as men hurried to don their harness, pikes clattered, but there was no sound yet of battle.

"Blow battle assembly," Mar yelled.

"They were supposed to be at least half a day's march away," James said. The horn blew again in warning. Squires led hastily saddled mounts in the moist dawn chill and knights buckled on their swords as they ran. When Sanderis dashed up, James said, "My armor, and be fast about it." Douglas strode out of the rags of mist, already armed and helm under his arm, with a man-at-arms at his side. "What's happened?" James asked him.

"The fat traitor is less lazy than I expected. He's stolen a march on us," Douglas said and thrust his chin at the man-at-arms, whose face James couldn't make out in the darkness. "The move scouts reported toward Lennox was a feint."

"My lord..." the man stuttered. "Mayhap they didn't expect sentries so far out. We spotted them a mile up the road toward Dumbarton. They're making a quick march this way. We signaled, but I ran as fast as I could be to bring news."

"We have little time, then," Mar growled and hurried back into his pavilion.

James' squire put his gilded cuirass on him as a servant helped fasten the buckles and clasps. "Hurry," James snapped. He was quickly into the cuisses that covered his thighs, the gorget, greaves, and pointed steel boots. As Sanderis fastened the close helm into place, one of the men-at-arms led up the huge destrier, a beautiful black that he had brought with him from England, for such horses were rare in Scotland.

Harooo! The horn blared again. War! Danger!

"I'll form the men ready to ride," Mar called and shoved his squire out of the way. His battered steel plate was topped with only a simple surcoat with a blue and white Stewart check and a bar sinister for his bastard birth. A groom ran up with his dun courser, not as heavy as James' mount but more maneuverable, and he leapt onto the animal to begin pointing their men into position.

James swung into the saddle and Sanderis handed him up his shield. "Do you want your lance, sire?" the squire asked. James looked down at him, shook his head, and commanded that the lad arm himself but stay out of the battle as much as he could. He snapped the visor down with a clang, wheeled his destrier, and trotted off. He cursed himself that they'd allowed the rebels to steal a march, and his stomach clenched into a hard knot. If they could, they would kill him in this battle. Killing him was the point of the entire endeavor. Then Joan and the baby would be next as Walter made sure there were no more obstacles to prevent his stealing the throne.

He rode past servants scrambling to strike the pavilions. Molten gold spread across the horizon with the first rays of the sun, yet the western sky was still velvet black with stars like a spill of diamonds across it. He wondered if he would live to see the stars this night. But he had to. He imagined tiny Margaret in the hands of his enemy and knew that he must not die.

War horns, many of them, sounded in the distance with a bloodcurdling note. Lord John Scrymgeour had raised James' banner and turned his horse to canter to his side. Their few dozen archers were trotting to place themselves behind the foot soldiers and forming a double line. The pikemen were forming two schiltrons, squares of double ranks with the pikes of the inner rank bristling over the outer rank's shoulder. One schiltron was under the Stewart banner of

Alexander of Mar and the other under the three white stars and crowned heart of the Douglas.

On the right, their small contingent of heavy horse, only a hundred but what they had, was forming and riding to join them. James used his sword to wave to Mar and Douglas, who were still shouting orders to their pikemen before they also joined the horse, since mounted they would be worse than useless.

A night march had to be wearing. James though surely it would put the rebels at a disadvantage, but the Highlanders were tough, savage fighters. Everyone said so. Soon Mar and Douglas thundered up to join the horse, their bannermen following. "Will they charge with their heavy horse?" James asked. That's what the French would do, but he'd never fought Highlanders.

Mar snorted derisively. "No, they'll use their Lochaber axes to tear apart the schiltrons and to rip the bellies out of our horses if they can. This will be dirty fighting. Not like the fancy French." He snapped down his visor.

"One day I'll tell you how fancy the French fight. But first I hope to live through today." James slashed a few times, warming up his sword arm. He stood in his stirrups. Trees dotted the rolling ground, but near the river it was a boggy marsh. A layer of mist still clung to the river, the blue, glassy water eddying past underneath.

"They'll have to attack the schiltrons first," Mar said, "so once they're engaged, we'll take them from the flank." He gave James a hard look, and James knew the man wondered if he was up to the task. "I mean to see that we kill more of them than they do of us, but that will be bloody work."

James heard a roll of drumbeats drawing near, and a thundering in his ears took up the cadence. Had he taken leave of his senses to meet his foes with such a small force, too few pikemen, too few archers, far too few heavy horse? He could have made them attack him in Stirling, lay siege to the castle. Except then his forces would have been trapped. He couldn't let that happen.

Then the enemy was running, screeching bloodcurdling war cries and ululating shouts. Afoot, the bare-legged Highlanders in their short kilts leapt and bound in their charge. Their axes were five feet long, and the blades with an evil hook on the end glittered in the sun as they slashed. Like a flood at the tide, they washed against the thin lines of pikemen. The armored heavy horse should turn the battle, but they were outnumbered, badly, and the rebels were on their home ground. A wedge would have worked in another battle but would have slashed into their own men here, so Mar had spread the horse into a long line. He gave James a thumbs up, and James nodded.

He raised his sword over his head and brought it down with a slash as he shouted, "Attack!" He slashed his horse with his spurs. It plunged to a gallop.

He rode knee to knee with Douglas and Mar down the slight incline, their heavy horses picking up speed as they went. James' banner streamed golden and red from Scrymgeour's staff, the rampant lion seeming to slash with its claws as it rippled. Ahead, the battle was a seething chaos as the Highlanders and pikemen hacked at each other.

James turned his head, trying to see through the narrow slit in his helm to find the rebel leaders. Those of certainty would be ahorse. James' stallion jumped over a body, hooves churning the dry earth and clods flying. James lifted his sword, shouting, "Scotland! Scotland!" as he hacked from behind through the neck of one of the attackers, and the force of his charging horse took the man's head from his body.

Douglas drove his lance through the bare chest of a Highlander, lifting him from his feet before the lance snapped.

Ahead through the seething mass of the battle was a small knot of mounted men with the Stewart banner fluttering over their heads. At last, was James' first thought. Indeed, Johne is as fat as they say. He was as big around as two barrels and sat astride a horse as huge as any James had ever seen. But first James had to stay alive to reach them, for the enemy was upon him, and he was surrounded. He hacked right and left with huge scything sweeps of his sword.

A Highlander lashed out at James' horse with his axe, and James knocked it aside. The man darted back for another try. James jerked on his reins, his horse reared, lashing out with iron-shod hooves. He rode the man down. Douglas was surrounded by three foes, but he took one down with a slash and raked the second across the neck with a backslash. John Scrymgeour dropped the point of his staff and drove it and James' banner through a Highlander's chest.

James urged his horse back into motion, jumping it over a scatter of corpses, some rebels and some his own men. The schiltron surged forward in an attempt to throw back the attackers. "To me!" James shouted to the other horsemen. "To me!" And he pressed toward the leaders of the rebels. Mar and the others were beside him again, and they were off. "Douglas! Douglas!" the earl cried as they rode. Let him as long as he is on my side, James thought whilst he had time.

His arm ached already from the continual slashing. Only a few followed him, the rest dead or tangled in the madness of the fighting. He wrestled his horse to keep it heading toward the banner that waved over the battle. The horse dodged another slashing axe and kicked someone's head. "Stewart!" he shouted. "Scotland!"

Another axeman ran at him. James lopped off the head of the axe and then his arm. The man sank shrieking to his knees as another tried to hook his axe under the destrier's belly. Mar's courser kicked in the man's chest, and he went sprawling. Douglas raised his mace to point beyond a small knot of heaving men. "Your Grace, look." It was Johne the Fat, surrounding by a score of mounted knights. Beside Johne was a thin man in armor with an ornate gold cross hanging from his neck, the bishop, James thought.

A thrown axe came tumbling at James from the left and thunked off his shield. He ignored it and rode hard toward Johne and his company. His cousin met him with a scream of rage, and their destriers slammed together. James wondered that any horse could carry the man but had no time for more when his cousin slammed a blow into James' shield, shouting. "Die! Die, usurper!"

James hacked at his cousin's head and shoulders. Steel clanged and grated upon steel. James realized the man was slow but strong as an ox. Where were the others? He couldn't see them in the narrow slit of his helm and daren't turn his head to look. "Die, damn you," Johne snarled, chopping savagely at James' shield. James pulled back on his reins and signaled his destrier to rear; its hooves slashed in Johne's face.

The man jerked back just in time, but James saw the flash of an axe in the edge of his vision. His horse screamed and twisted, trying to escape the pain. James jerked his feet free of the stirrups to leap free, but it was too late. He was falling. He kicked his foot over the saddle so it wouldn't be crushed. His shoulder hit the ground with a sickening thud. Groaning, he couldn't see past the flashes of blinding white light. He dragged himself a few feet on the hard, torn earth. A horse was above him. He looked, stomach churning with pain, at its brown belly. It was immense. His head spun, but he pawed at his empty scabbard. Then he heard the man on the horse shouting, "Douglas! To me! A Douglas!" James rolled onto his side and tried to get to his knees, but pain jolted through his shoulder. His stomach roiled and his mouth filled with bile. He held his breath so he wouldn't throw up inside his helm.

Somewhere a trumpet blew. There were more shouts and screams and the thunder of horses' hooves, but he couldn't quite take it all in.

Dazed, James looked up to see Douglas shielding him on one side and Mar on the other. Beneath the feet of Mar's horse lay James the Fat's Stewart banner. He blinked at it, confused. When he tried to stand, pain hammered through his shoulder, but he managed to lurch to his feet. He looked around and the battle had ceased. "We've won?" he croaked and lifted his visor. The movement nearly put him on his knees from the pain.

"A victory of sorts," Mar said with a scowl. "They're running. When you went down, they got Johne away."

"Why aren't you chasing them then?"

"Keeping you alive was more important," Mar pointed out.

James meant to thank him, but instead when he opened his mouth, he spewed on the ground. He wiped his mouth with the back of his hand. "I thank you, my lord, for my life, but pursue them, by all the saints. Take your own men, and Douglas may bide here with me."

Mar saluted him with a bloody sword and shouted to his herald. The trumpets sounded again as he rode to gather his men.

There were groans from the injured and dying Highlanders left behind by the retreat. A knight was ridding down a fleeing man who tossed away his axe as he ran to splash into the river. A pikeman kicked over a body he was looting. Bodies were being dragged by the feet into a pile. A loud moaning was suddenly cut off with the hack of a pike. One of his men knelt over a body, cursing.

"I need another horse." James had liked that destrier and another would be expensive to come by, but it was best not to become over-fond of warhorses. By the time they found a courser and brought it to him, Mar's force had swept from the field following the trail of the rebels.

With his shoulder throbbing inside his armor, James climbed carefully into the saddle. He and Douglas rode over the battlefield looking over their losses. Many were dead; pikemen had died by the hundred, for Lochaber axes were terrible in their efficiency. Bodies lay in pools of congealing blood, their thighs and bellies ripped open. The clerics had already set up a small tent and were helping to bandage the wounded. John Scrymgeour was nursing a dagger slash across his face. The earl of Angus limped to them, his leg nearly crushed when his horse, like James', was cut out from under him. James sighed. Of the thousand men who had ridden into battle with him, he thought perhaps half had survived.

"You'd best have that shoulder put right," Douglas said, "if it is to heal."

James nodded. He was sure it was dislocated rather than broken, but putting it back into place was going to hurt worse than having it set. He would have it tended, but first he turned to the earl. "I'll be no warrior king. It is best you should know that. I fight when I must, but..." He took a deep breath. "I hate this business."

Douglas shrugged. "Mayhap you shan't have many battles to fight, but I'd lay no wagers on it."

Listing to one side, his shoulder and arm thrumming with pain, James turned his horse's head and rode toward the tent where clerics bent over the wounded, winding bandages around bloody limbs.

Chapter Fifteen

MAY 15, 1425

The Great Hall of Stirling Castle was muggy with heat from the warm May day, but much of the warmth was from the close press of bodies; the scent of lavender, musk, and orris root combined with the smell of sweat into a cloying fug. Every nobleman, churchman, and burgher qualified for parliament was packed into the vast chamber. The whitewashed stone walls were covered with hunting tapestries, but behind the throne hung a banner as huge as a ship's sail of the royal standard being held by two rampant white unicorns.

When James entered, the guards slammed shut the doors and crossed their pikes. He glanced briefly at the gallery screen, where Joan and her ladies watched. The crown was heavy on his head, and he felt a trickle of sweat run from beneath it, but the honors of Scotland must show the severity of the acts to be taken this day, so he gripped the scepter in his hand and strode solemnly up the narrow aisle to the dais. The hall was remarkably quiet. Someone coughed and there was a soft shuffling of feet. He passed the row of the assize of twenty-one nobles who would pass judgment on Lord Walter

Stewart. All but two of the earls of the kingdom and fourteen knights would decide the traitors' fates.

The great officers of state were already in position around the throne. John Scrymgeour leaned a bit on the staff of the banner he held, his face pasty from a wound fever and the slash on his face red and puckered. William Hay stood to the side holding before him the Sword of State. Robert de Keith stood next to the throne with his hand on the hilt of his sword, the only man in the hall to be allowed one other than the guards. James nodded to Bishop Wardlaw, who stood before a throne nearly as ornate as that of the king's, and sat in the heavy throne.

The prisoners stood in a line at the side of the room, but the guards surrounding them and the chains on their hands did not detract from their finery. All four were as well clad as anyone in the room in silk doublets and hose. A place was left empty for Johne the Fat, who had managed to flee pursuit for Ireland. Walter Stewart sat apart from the others because his was to be the first trial. He glared at James, his dark eyes seething with not a sign of fear, and his head was tilted at an arrogant angle.

The chancellor banged his gavel on the table where the Great Seal lay displayed. He cleared his throat, and James wished he could have spared the man this. His face was so gray and his hands had such a tremor that James wasn't sure he could keep to his feet for the long day ahead of them. But after pausing to look over the parliament, he said in a clear voice, "I bring before you the indictment of Lord Walter Stewart. He stands accused of high treason in that he stated the intent to rule the realm; in that he refused to swear fealty to his rightful king and lord; in that he conspired with others to take up arms against his king and lord; in that he planned and intended regicide. Of all this we do have witnesses to attest."

When the chancellor called Alan of Otterburn, Murdoch made a choked sound and looked around with a certain wide-eyed desperation. Even Walter's lips thinned, but otherwise his expression didn't change as the rangy man with ginger hair down to his shoulders was brought in. His Adam's apple bobbed, but he answered Lauder's questions calmly enough. Aye, he had written letters addressed to Walter Stewart planning the king's death and his father taking the throne to name Walter as regent. When Lauder held out letters taken from Walter in his dungeon in Bass Rock Castle, Otterburn nodded sharply and agreed those were ones he had written. Aye, the letters had been given to Sir John Montgomery to carry. Aye, letters had been exchanged with the earl of Lennox, Sir Johne Stewart, and the Bishop of Argyll to plan the uprising.

James sat unmoving, cold as ice as he listened to the testimony of their plans for his murder. It had been no more calculatingly planned than that of his brother so many years before, and at the same hands, though the old man was dead. James would have raged, but instead he felt frozen. None of this was new, yet hearing the planning of it that had taken a year made him so cold that he thought he might never warm. And he looked at the faces in the parliament and had to wonder... Were these truly all who had conspired? Were there others who plotted foul treason and murder?

Brought in, the hulking John Montgomery of Ardrossan confessed that he had subverted one of the guards at Bass Rock Castle to carry letters. "I dinnae read, my lords," he insisted looking around at the serious faces. "How could I ken what was in the letters they gave me?"

Many in the hall had heard Walter claim the throne for his father before James had him imprisoned at Bass Rock, but Thomas Myrton stood to testify to it.

At the end, given the chance to defend himself, Walter

surged to his feet with a hoarse laugh. "You accuse me when it is you who have no right to the throne. It was my father who should have been king, never yours."

There were gasps and a few whispers. The Albanys had always claimed that James' grandfather's marriage was not valid, but the Church had not agreed. James slowly shook his head. How many had died and how long had he suffered for this heedless, foolish claim?

"Enough," the chancellor said, banging his gavel. "If you have a defense, we will hear it, but this treason is no defense, and we shall not suffer it."

Murdoch was nothing if not arrogant. James gave him that much because he threw back his head and proclaimed, "I do not admit this man's right to try me. Now I have naught more to say." His back stiff with pride, he sat back down.

James clutched the arms of the throne but otherwise moved not a muscle as Lauder polled the assize.

"My lords, it is now your duty before King James and the Estates of Scotland to give your verdict on the charges against Lord Walter Stewart. Guilty or innocent? My lord Earl of Atholl."

"Guilty," Atholl rapped out in a gruff voice.

"My lord Earl of Douglas."

"Guilty," said the impassive Douglas.

Mar had just ridden in the night before from where his men were laying siege to Inchmurrin Castle, where Lennox's sons were proclaiming defiance, and he looked tired and worn, but he rapped out a quick, "Guilty."

The grim tally went on, each man called on. Although the entire parliament was gathered, only the twenty-one members of the assize were called upon for a verdict. Every one of them gave a guilty verdict. James let out a breath he hadn't realized he was holding, but his eyes were fixed on the man who had so desperately wanted him dead. Walter Stewart's face had never changed, though he'd drawn his hands into tight fists. He was no coward, traitor though he was.

William Lauder's voice wavered a bit, and James saw that he looked at the far wall rather than at the prisoner as he said, "There is only one thing that I—as Chancellor and Keeper of the Great Seal of Scotland—can do. It is not a matter of choice. Only one duty now devolves upon me:

"It is ordered by the parliament of Scotland that you, Walter Stewart, suffer the punishment of death by having your head struck from your body at the place known as Heading Hill this day. This is the sentence of the law of Scotland."

Murdoch gave a strangled cry, and there was a low murmur that went through the whole chamber like a wave in a lake. A single voice somewhere in the crowd called out a low, "Our Lady forfend." When Lauder turned toward him, James feared the frail man might collapse. He almost reached a hand toward him but stopped himself when Lauder steadied himself and said, "I command that the officers of state carry out this sentence forthwith unless his King's Grace commands that his will is otherwise."

James tore his gaze from Lauder and fixed it upon the far wall. His grip on the arms of the throne turned his knuckles white. He fixed his mouth into a hard line and said nothing.

After a moment, Lauder said, "Then justice shall be done. This parliament is adjourned until tomorrow for the trial of the other accused. God save the king!"

James managed to pry his fingers loose and stood with a jerk. He turned and strode out the rear door without ever having said a word. His jaw was clenched so tight he wasn't sure he could have.

Chapter Sixteen

James wasn't sure if he should be glad or sorry that Walter Stewart died as arrogantly as he had lived. The duke brushed past the priest who accompanied him and swaggered to the stone at the top of Heading Hill. His glance at James was almost taunting.

The crowd was utterly silent. The priest clutched at Walter's cloak and said something, but the prisoner shook him off. The lords, knights, burghers, and servants moved aside as the headsman trod past, tall and with arms like tree trunks, his face hidden by a hood. James heard a woman scream somewhere in the crowd. The priest fell to his knees, running his rosary beads through his fingers.

The afternoon was hot, and sweat pooled under James' arms like a swamp. Clutching his hands into fists, he forced his face to blankness. He must not show what he felt, although God in Heaven, he wasn't sure what he felt. Despair, perhaps, but emotions roiled through him like water at the boil so confused he could not tell one from another. This was his duty. But how could he relish it so? When had he become so much like Henry of Monmouth? He thought his neck might snap, so tightly were his muscles clenched.

At the heading stone, the headsman gestured and Walter Stewart knelt. He brushed his hair out of the way. As the headsman raised the axe with both hands high above his head, its curved blade glistened in the bright sunlight.

The headsman did his job well and took the head off with a single blow. Crimson sprayed across the grass. The head bounced and then rolled, and James could not take his eyes off it. The heat had gone out of the day, and once again he felt cold all through. He swallowed hard. He would have to send the headsman a reward, he thought, as he returned to the castle trailed by his officers of state. No one spoke to him. Perhaps his expression was grim enough to deter them.

He would have spared Joan his mood if he could, but there was nothing to do but return to the royal apartments. She waved out her two ladies, both Douglases, and poured him a goblet of wine. He sipped it as he paced around the chamber touching the hangings and the papers on the table, trying to ground himself where he was and put the sight of that head bounding across the grass out of his mind. He had killed men before often enough. But never had he been forced to execute someone, even a mortal enemy. He should have felt...something that he did not. Sorrow? Rage? Instead he felt empty, as though he had lost his very self. The morrow would be even worse.

"You haven't eaten all day," Joan said. "You'll feel more yourself when you do."

"I shall not feel myself until this is done. And mayhap not then." He continued his course, circling the room, and stopped before the cold hearth to run fingers over the stone.

"What do you mean?" She sounded confused. Did she not know what would come next?

He turned, his face oaken as it had been all day. "They must all die. It is the only way the realm will ever be safe."

She gasped. "The whole family? Surely not, James."

"You think Duke Murdoch is less guilty than Walter? We know better. Lennox was part of the plan. Even Alexander, whom I knighted, joined them knowing it was treason. And they meant murder. Of me. Of you and the bairn. Of anyone who stood between them and the throne."

She was shaking her head. "James, not the whole family. I beg you." She wrung her hands. "Duke Murdoch, yes. He is as guilty as Sir Walter, but not the others. Lennox is an old man. Make him forfeit his lands. That will pull his fangs. The same with young Alexander."

"Fangs," James repeated thoughtfully. "That is a good word. They are a nest of asps, and if I leave any alive, more will only breed."

She darted to grasp his arm. "I beseech you, beg you. Think what people will say of you if you have them all killed. They'll say it was greed. They'll say terrible things about you. Think terrible things."

"And will you think them too, my love?" His chest felt hollow and empty as though the heart was gone out of him. "The parliament will bring its sentence, as is its right. They have no choice. And I will not show them any more mercy than they showed my brother. Than they would have shown me. Or you."

She moved her mouth but could not seem to find more words. James shook his head and gently took her hand from his arm. The day had left him weary beyond words, but he knew that sleep would elude him. He strode out of the chamber. That night James paced the towers and parapets of Stirling Castle, staring often into the dark blue sky. Not once did he close his eyes.

On the morn, parliament resumed to hear the evidence

against the three remaining accused. It was a repeat of the previous day. James stared above their heads, withdrawn and impassive. His face was even more still than the day before. Again the twenty-one men in the jury repeated a chorus of "guilty" when Bishop Lauder called upon them. When Lauder asked him the customary question as to mercy, his eyes twitched, but he held his breath until it was over.

At the Heading Hill, Duke Murdoch stumbled to his death, shaking, but he made no sound. Alexander fought as he was dragged up by the guards and pushed down upon with his head over the edge of the beheading stone. Then he went limp. But Lennox cursed every step of the way, his thin face twisted with malice. Even as the headsman's axe descended, he was cursing James.

James felt hollowed out. Empty. He turned his back on the bloody ground. That night he again spent on the ramparts, leaning his elbows on the rough stone and staring into the sky. Twice servants came to beg him to eat, but he only shook his head. He supposed Joan had sent them. He felt weary far beyond his years and could only hope he would eventually be weary enough to sleep and that she would not reproach him. Because he had done nothing more than had to be done. He would do it again, so he didn't understand why he kept seeing a spray of crimson gushing across the grass and gore dripping down the stone.

Chapter Seventeen

The sun felt wonderfully warm, and the rustle and occasional squawk of ducks in the reeds, the faint rustle of the waters of the loch, and the slow, sweet trill of a warbler in the trees soothed her. The sun made the tranquil water shimmer like a sheet of beaten silver. James stood akimbo as he listened to the master mason, who was pointing and gesticulating about the rebuilding of Linlithgow Palace. On this side, the wall had collapsed completely, the stones in a blackened jumble over fallen timbers.

Joan smiled as Margaret toddled up to her father and clasped onto his leg when she stumbled. He stopped to beam down at her, and Joan felt the stirrings of happiness for the first time in months. The fire that had ravaged the palace and nearby Kirk of St. Michael might be a blessing, for it had given James something to think about other than his melancholy over destroying half of his own family. Not once had he expressed regret, but for months he had not slept more than a few hours. And Joan had for a while been sure he hadn't forgiven her for her words to him, but he still came to her bed even if he lay there for hours awake. Not once had she reproached him for the executions. If the subject came up, he simply shrugged and said he'd done what must be done. But he wasn't himself. William Lauder's death had been such a blow. Joan wondered if James felt alone, yet she was there for him.

She laid a hand on the slight swell of her belly when there was a nudge. Indeed, she thought they were both beginning to recover from the horrors of the Albany insurrection.

Margaret loosed her father's leg and toddled toward a bird pecking in the grass, giggling with delight. "Bird!" she crowed. James' gaze met Joan's and a grin slit his face. Yes, rebuilding the palace was just what he needed, and she would love a place to call home.

James was pacing out the area where he wanted the new great hall of the palace to be as the master made notes. He chuckled when Margaret came padding after him again. He had squatted and pointed toward a couple of starlings hunting bugs in the weeds when a mounted party of men approached, two in fine clerics' garb and a score of men-at-arms. James continued to point toward the birds as they chuckled and whistled, but he watched the two dismount and approach, his expression growing stern.

Bishop Henry Wardlaw's hair was now completely white and his jowls hung loose, but his shoulders were still broad and his step firm. The light gleamed on the dark brocade of his cassock and the gold of belt and purse at his waist. John Cameron made a stark contrast in his simpler garb, still thin and the hair around his tonsure dark, as they walked, keeping some distance apart. Joan took a deep breath and steeled herself before she stood.

Margaret stopped and gave the two a serious look before she pointed and said loudly, "Bird!" The starlings took off with a murmuration that made the child howl in laughter.

Joan strolled toward them, watching a bit uneasily as Cameron bowed to first the king and then to her.

At last James stood from his crouch and said, "A fine day for a ride, but I suppose you had a greater purpose than that."

Cameron's look was troubled, but he motioned to Bishop Wardlaw with a small bow. The old man looked from James to Cameron and back again.

James gave an impatient grunt. "I have no secrets from my secretary, Reverence. Do you have news for me? Then tell me."

"Very well, Your Grace." Wardlaw sighed. "I have received a response from His Holiness the Pope to your appointment of John Cameron as Bishop of Glasgow."

"And...?"

"His Holiness reminds you that the see is reserved and only he may make the appointment. He has quashed the election of the Glasgow Chapter and declared it invalid." Wardlaw gave Cameron a cool glance, and Joan wondered if Wardlaw's opposition to the appointment was based on jealousy. She hadn't thought so, for John Cameron was a bastard of low birth. Many had opposed it, insulted that one of the many clerics of higher birth wasn't chosen. One of those had been Bishop Wardlaw, but James had insisted. He trusted Cameron more than anyone else, possibly even more than Wardlaw, whose insistence that only clerics should attend the new University of St. Andrews set them at odds. There had been times when the two had even shouted at each other, and James became so angry he couldn't speak to the Primate.

Margaret had sat in the grass and plucked a handful of honeysuckle that she was eating, so Joan circled the three men. She knelt and pointed to another bird to the child. She loved birds so much. As the babe babbled on, Joan continued to listen.

"And I remind you that I do not admit that the Pope has the right to appoint bishops within my realm."

"The see of Glasgow is reserved, Sire. I warned you as much. The other sees you may appoint, but not the sees of Glasgow or St. Andrews. Only the Pope may make those appointments."

The king's face was flushed. He swept his arm wide as he exclaimed, "And how will he stop me?"

His glance at Wardlaw was knowing. Joan suspected he had long since understood why Wardlaw opposed him and decided how to handle it. She had little doubt Cameron had the most agile mind in Scotland, even more than James.

Cameron said mildly, "Sire, I would have no dissention with the Holy See over my appointment. I am sure there is some way to bring the Pope to your will given time. Sending envoys to the Holy See might be the solution. Thomas Myrton has often acted for you in the past, has he not, Sire? As Archdeacon of Dunkeld as he is now..." He shrugged. "But for the nonce, there is another matter I must raise with you."

"Another matter?" James asked, sounding annoyed at Cameron trying to change the topic. "What then?"

"I received on your behalf earlier today a letter from Sir Robert Umfraville. He makes numerous complaints concerning violations of the truce and charges Scots with the molesting of the English forces that hold Berwick and Roxburgh. Indeed, he was most indignant. But the main matter was the payment of ransom."

James plunged his hands into his hair. "We have paid... How much, John?"

"Four thousand merks altogether."

James paced back and forth a few times. "We simply do not have the funds to pay more. What merks are in the treasury, and it is not many, must go for the rebuilding of Linlithgow. The burghs are to make a payment, but that shan't be soon. What of the hostages? There is to be an exchange. Might the English refuse?"

"The hostages have been brought north from the Tower to Knaresborough and Pontefract, but Umfraville hints—only hints—that the release will be delayed if more funds are not received."

James glanced at Wardlaw, who shook his head. They had already received funds from the church, and more would not be forthcoming. Wardlaw had already said as much, and the disputes between the two men had not softened his stance.

James paced a few more times back and forth. "They make me bargain like a merchant. Holy Rood, I need you as my chancellor, John. That means I need you confirmed as bishop."

Having tired herself out, Margaret had curled up in a patch of grass and was peacefully sleeping, so Joan stood. "With a child king, the English are in no position to press you, are they? Especially since the war in France is not going well." The Maid of Orleans was said to have the will of God on her side. Joan wasn't sure if it was true, but reports said the English had lost several important battles.

"What of the Auld Alliance?" Wardlaw asked. "Since Douglas's and Buchan's deaths, nothing more has been said of supporting France, but that would give the English pause."

"Sending them an army would cost even more than paying the ransom and might well be useless. Charles has never even been crowned. He's been driven hither and yon like a coursed stag since his mad father died. Besides, I have nae desire to end up at war with the English. We simply must maintain the truce."

Joan put her hand on his arm and squeezed. Please God, that would not happen for any English army her brothers would be likely to lead. "There must be something short of that." She turned to Cameron. "What do you think, Master Cameron?"

"The French position is stronger than it once was. It's rumored that the Dauphin has finally decided to be crowned. An embassy to him would be wise, I believe, and be sure it is known to the English. Even a hint of renewing the alliance might be enough of a threat to buy the time that we need. It may be that we could stretch out negotiations for an alliance with the French for a number of years. Why not? And with the French position strengthening, I believe we may force the English to dance to our tune, or at least to cease trying to make us dance to theirs."

"I doubt that an embassage to the French would cause sufficient alarm to achieve your goal," Wardlaw said.

"If the envoys proposed a marriage between Dauphin Louis and young Margaret, it might."

"She is still a babe," Joan exclaimed. Joan gave James a determined look. "I know I had more choice than she will be allowed, but I shall not lose her so young."

"Your Grace, I meant only that we should propose it and make sure that the English hear of the idea. Mayhap even make a formal promise, but nothing more."

Joan breathed a soft sigh of relief when James nodded. "Of course, my love. It shall be many years before we even consider allowing her out of our sight." He gave the sleeping child a doting look. Even Bishop Wardlaw nodded in agreement.

Chapter Eighteen

JULY 1428

The air was warm and heavy with the scent of heather, and the land had a beauty that James had never seen in the south. It was years beyond counting since any King of the Scots had set foot in this part of the realm. James dared not do so without an army at his back. The fact chafed. He was determined to bring this fair land into unity under his reign. In truth, he had not suspected its beauty. They only said it was a wild and savage place. Riding down the long slopes of moors dotted with broom and yellow gorse, he was speechless at the sight that stretched out before him. Beyond the moors was a checkered scene of woodlands and pastures that led to the slate roofs of Inverness huddled around the castle. On one side, a loch stretched gleaming away out of sight, and above all the massive peaks of purple mountains arose into the clouds.

They traveled in a river of polished steel, a force three hundred strong of knights and lords and men-at-arms in chainmail. Forty days before, he had sent summons to parliament to his castle of Inverness.

The ride from Aberdeen to Inverness had been hard,

crossing the hills of the Mounth with not only his court but a large enough force to repel a possible attack. Nerves had been on edge, and every day had seen quarrels that he had quashed with a harsh hand and threats of severe fines. He had allowed only two of the queen's ladies-in-waiting to accompany them. More would have made the journey even more of a trial. White mules pulled a litter for the queen's comfort in the warm summer sun, but when the heat eased, Joan often chose to ride by his side on her beautiful cream palfrey that she had ridden the day that they wed.

James had known very well that this trip was a risk. Rebellion was mother's milk in the mountains of Scotland. And in the past few years, the violence and fighting had grown even worse, with feud and sack causing suffering across every village and town. This was his realm, and he would see that it ceased or die trying. Once the clan MacDonald had held total sway, but they had been weakened to the point that instead there was almost anarchy. That James might die to bring peace caused him before he left Perth to cause the Estates to take an oath of fealty to the queen and left behind both Margaret and the infant Isabella in safe hands at Edinburgh Castle. It was a vast, colorful cavalcade under dozens of banners that surrounded that of the king. It almost looked peaceable until you saw that they had left behind the servants, minstrels, cooks and brought no wagons of comforts. Every man rode fully armed.

James rode at the head of the column with Joan by his side, flanked by the Earl of Douglas on one side and the Earl of Mar on the other. Mar grumbled under his breath as they approached the city. He had opposed this entire venture as foolhardy. No parliament had ever been held in the Highlands. When they rode into Inverness, the streets were crowded with men in tartans of every color, all armed. Joan edged her horse close to his side, but other than stares, they rode peacefully through the castle gates. Mar was quickly shouting out orders for their own men to man the gates. James slept with a blade at his side that night.

The next day was all noise and confusion as the castle servants were set to preparing the great hall for the parliament. Fresh rushes were laid, sweetened with heather, the long trestle tables removed, and benches put in place. James sat on the dais with John Cameron by his side, and they discussed the few matters to be brought up. James sipped at a goblet of wine as John went over them and allowed the Highlanders, who had never attended parliament in the south, to look him over. All the day, men swaggered in, Highland lairds of the Mactaggarts, Frasers, Gordons, Gunns, Macphersons, MacEwans, Munros, and the like, answering his summons to parliament. James greeted them with a nod; these were not the ones James waited for, however. He chewed his lip and exchanged looks with his secretary. He must bring the great chiefs to the parliament and make them feel the weight of the royal authority. He had thrown the die, and if he lost, he could not guarantee they could win their way back south of the Firth of Forth.

James knew he could show no nerves, so he lay awake in the dark beside Joan again that night, his blade beside their bed. In the morning, they broke their fast together, and he forced himself to patience. The Parliament would open at Terce. James was dressing in his finest doublet, cloth of gold, the sleeves slashed with crimson silk, when a cacophony from below in the town broke out. It was shouts and the skirling of bagpipes, and to be heard within the castle, it had to be a great many people. James took a deep breath. A guard knocked and stuck his head in to say that the Earl of Mar was without. When he entered, James just raised his eyebrows in question.

"It is a substantial host, Sire, under the MacDonald

banner. It is Alexander of Islay right enough and hundreds of his caterans."

"Hundreds." James scowled. That was in direct contravention of the law, and they were throwing it in his face. "Do they appear peaceable?"

"They're not in battle array. They remain outwith the town, but beyond that I cannae say."

"Alexander of the Isles would not come alone. What other banners?"

"I spied the banners of Macruri and MacArthur and Campbell, but there are at least a dozen others."

James let out a long breath. He grasped Joan's hand for a moment. James had not dared risk bringing the regalia on so dangerous a venture, but he donned a gold coronet to serve as a crown. He twitched a smile at Mar that felt more like a grimace. "You've fought the Donalds before, my lord, so if we must, and I trust you."

"Aye, I had a victory of sorts at Harlaw against this one's father." Mar snorted. "But we were prepared for battle."

"You've seen to ample guards for the great hall?" At Mar's assent, James raised his chin. "Today we are prepared for a parliament, then, so let us hie to it." He strode for the door.

Since John Cameron could not act as Chancellor until he was consecrated as bishop, and their envoys were still in Rome, the Marischal took the roll call and James introduced the first subject for discussion: the compensation of churches when their lands were destroyed by feuding. The cathedral of Elgin was still being rebuilt from the destruction by the Wolf of Badenach, the present Earl of Mar's father.

Columba de Dunbar, the Bishop of Elgin, was making a passionate plea that Mar had a duty to compensate further for his father's depredations. As Mar scowled at the bishop's comments, there was a commotion at the door, and it was thrown open with a crash. The bishop paused, open mouthed, at the interruption and turned to stare at the late arrivals.

In the lead was a wiry, red-haired man, dressed as finely as any other noble in the room in silk doublet and hose girded at the waist by a heavy belt of solid gold and a sword at his hip. James nodded to Alexander of Islay, Earl of Ross and high chief of Clan MacDonald. Alexander had been one of those who had voted for the death of the Albanys but since had consistently refused to attend parliament.

"I understand your concern, Your Reverence," James said to the bishop, "but I suspect that his lordship the Earl of Mar may take another view. It was after all his father, not himself, who raided the cathedral, as reprehensible as that action was."

The Earl of Mar jumped to his feet. "I do indeed, Sire. That act was not of my doing and occurred during a time of great lawlessness in the realm after the death of the late king's father. It is too late to bring up acts that occurred so long ago."

"Have there been raids more recently?" James asked, knowing quite well that there had been. Other than his nod, he had refused to acknowledge the newcomers, and Alexander of Islay stood, red faced, while the score of lairds behind him glared angrily.

Glancing uneasily toward the Earl of Ross, William de Blare, Abbot of Kinloss, rose to his feet. "Kinloss Abbey itself has suffered raids. As Your Grace knows, we have had the valuable salmon fishing rights on the River Findhorn since the time of the great King Robert the Bruce, which you confirmed. However, we have been so harried by raiders that the rights now go unclaimed."

James almost laughed at the sight of everyone in the parliament trying to watch the Earl of Ross and his company where they had come to a stop in the middle of the great hall whilst trying not to be seen to be staring. Alexander seemed at a loss, thin lipped over his hawk nose.

"So there is no doubt that even now, raids and lawlessness exist in the north of the realm," James said mildly. "Leaving aside the question of further recompense for Elgin Cathedral—" James paused to nod to the bishop, who had to know no such thing would happen "—the salient issue seems to be how best to quell the lawlessness and maintain the king's peace in the realm. Mayhap the clan chiefs of each area should have the responsibility for not only their own clans but that of anyone in their lands."

James leaned back in his throne and allowed his gaze to rest on the Earl of Ross. "How say you, My Lord Earl? I bid you take your place and give me your advice on the matter. And mayhap the chiefs who accompany you would advise me as well."

The earl crossed his arms. "I dinnae come here to sit like a tame dog and listen to speeches, James Stewart. I came to speak with you privily on important matters, as did these lairds who accompany me."

"However, I summoned you to my parliament and my parliament you shall attend. I shall be pleased to speak with you privily later. Now take your seats." He turned his head to nod to Robert de Keith and said coolly, "Lord High Constable, you have your orders. No one shall enter or leave except by my express consent."

"Men!" William Hay shouted. "Bar the doors."

Men-at-arms in full armor stepped in front of the closed doors, eight-foot pikes in their hands.

Alexander of Islay spun on his heel and stepped toward the doors. For a long second, James held his breath. The Highlanders were outnumbered five to one by the guards who lined the room, and fully another hundred guards were outside on the walls, but none of the nobles in the room had more than a dirk at his belt in the midst of parliament.

Several of the clan chiefs around Ross turned in a slow circle as they surveyed the numbers of the guards. Several others dropped their hands to their hilts. There were grunts and curses until Ross said, "I want no bloodshed. I came to talk, nae to fight."

"Wise words, my lord. Now if you will take your places, I would hear your advice on this matter. My lords, give way so the newcomers may sit together if they so please."

Ross bowed to James with something of a flourish, giving way with some good grace. As there was shuffling and moving about on the benches, James motioned to the High Marischal. When Keith bent, James whispered for him to carry out the orders he already had. Keith slipped out by a side door and James turned back to the parliament.

James smiled slightly as he said, "This concerns you in particular my lords, which is why I chose to come north to hold the parliament. It seems to me that the powers of the clan chiefs in some respects are equal to that of the barons of the realm and in some respects lesser. I shall propose to parliament that they be made equal to establish better peace in the realm. What say you?"

Douglas jumped to his feet. "Your Grace, such a thing is unheard of! The privileges of the barons have come down from our fathers and their fathers and their fathers before them. Such privileges should not be lightly given to...to..." At Ross's narrow-eyed glare, Douglas seemed to rethink his words. "...to others."

"Not lightly, my lord," James said. "This is a serious matter that should be given due consideration. Do any of you have anything to add to the discussion?"

A beefy clan chief with reddish gold hair down to his

shoulders stood and said, "The power I hae in my own lands..."

James held up a hand with a raised eyebrow. "And you are, my lord?"

The man glowered as he said, "I am Alexander of Clanranald. Son of Godfrey, son of Donald."

James nodded affably. "You may continue."

"My rights as chief of Clanranald are nae business of any Lowlander, nae you, nor any other. My powers—" He flung a hand out. "All of our powers were handed down from our ancestors, and it's a matter for no one but myself."

James steepled his hands below his chin and nodded thoughtfully. He turned his gaze to Alexander. "And you, my lord, do you concur with Alexander of Clanranald that the crown has no right to increase your powers?"

Snorts of laughter came from the Lowlanders, some of whom slapped their knees in delight as Ross stood and looked around in frustration at the hubbub. With a pained look he said, "I have a' the powers I need in my own lands."

"I'll have order in the parliament," James said raising his voice to be heard. "This is no laughing matter, my lords. Now I want reasoned advice on the powers which the clan chiefs have to govern in their own lands and whether those powers should be increased for better governance."

Young MacKenneth of Kintail, a lanky boy of no more seventeen as James judged, stood and said that he thought more powers were a good idea, and he would welcome them. That garnered some glares from the older clan chiefs but began something that resembled a debate that went back and forth. The Highlanders were at first in the uncomfortable position of arguing against having greater powers since they would come from the crown, but in the face of seeming to agree with the disliked Lowland lords, they began to come over to agreeing with James.

After a time, Keith returned, whispered for several minutes in the king's ear, and took his place behind the throne.

James raised both hands to call for silence.

"My lords, I believe we have taken this as far as we may in one sitting. It is a difficult matter, so I bid you take time to think on it, and we shall return to the matter at a later parliament. However, another matter has been brought to my attention by the Lord High Marischal which, sadly, I cannot ignore. He has reported to me that certain members of parliament have brought with them large numbers of men, far more than were allowed by act of the first parliament of my reign. The numbers any man is allowed in his train are quite clearly laid out as being no more than twenty for an earl or a dozen for a lord or bishop. Yet I am informed that the numbers brought to Inverness number in the hundreds. This is a violation so great I cannae ignore it."

Alexander of Ross jumped to his feet. "You expect me to travel with no more than twenty men? That is madness!"

"My lord, it is the law of the realm. If you had objections, the time to make them was in the first parliament." James gave the man a sharp look since he had not attended that parliament. "All who offend in this matter are to be arrested and held until such time as it is the king's pleasure to release them. Hence, all here who have exceeded the number laid down are under arrest for the term of the parliament. At the cessation..."

Shouts drowned out the rest, so James leaned back in his throne and watched the chaos. Let them work out their rage, he thought, and they did, waving their arms and cursing. Several pushed their way to the center aisle, only to stand staring at the crossed pikes held by guards at the doors.

James doubted there was a clan chief in the room who had fewer than fifty men in his train.

After giving them time to vent their fury, James motioned for Lord Lyon to have the trumpets blown. Even that took several blares to quiet the pandemonium.

James stood and looked gravely down on the parliament. "For shame! This is a solemn parliament of the realm, and you treat is as though it were not better than a town market to shout and curse. Be seated and keep silent.

"I repeat. This arrest is merely token and for the length of the parliament. All are confined to the castle, but within it you are free men. Once the parliament is dismissed, your arrest will be ended. I can do no other without bringing my laws and parliament into disrepute. But do not mistake me, my lords. Any man whatsoever, however great he may be, who breaks the king's ward commits treason." He gave them a very long, silent look. "And the penalty for treason is death."

Chapter Nineteen

In the morning, James deemed it wise to make the remaining day of the parliament as boring as possible, so he brought up the dates of the close season for salmon fishing. However important the salmon were, the exact dates of the season were not likely to evoke high passion. He put to Alexander of Ross and the abbot of Kinloss whether the current dates were best suited for giving a high yield. It wasn't long before a servant came to whisper in the ear of the High Marischal. James flinched at William Keith's grim look as he came to bend to whisper, "One of the guards found a rope to the ground from the west wall."

James scanned the benches of the parliament. There were so many seated that he hadn't noticed a missing few. Now he saw that James Campbell of Lorne was not in their number. The number of Highland chiefs looked short by several more, but it was impossible for him to be sure who was missed, so he motioned to Cameron, who agreed that some were missing, and pointed out that Alexander Macruri and John MacArthur were both missing from the hall, but all else were present as far as he could tell.

"Search the castle. Be sure that those three are missing. Report back as soon as you are certain."

The debate had stalled as the members noticed the quiet discussion taking place on the dais, so James asked if they were agreed-upon dates for the close season. By the time further debate took place, since of course they did not agree, Keith returned to report that there was no sign of the three anywhere within the castle walls.

James took a very deep breath. Perhaps this was inevitable, but he had hoped to avoid it. He raised a hand to interrupt the abbot of Kinloss, who was arguing for a shorter close.

"My lords," he said gruffly. "The High Marischal has brought me serious news. Three clan chiefs, members of this parliament, held under arrest, have left my ward and fled this castle. They did this in full knowledge of the penalty proscribed. These men are Alexander Macruri of Clanranald, John MacArthur of Dunstaffnage, and James Campbell of Lorne. All three have flouted the law and my lawful royal command. This is high treason. The penalty for high treason is death. Has anyone any word to say in their defense? I would hear the advice of my parliament. Is there any reason to spare these miscreants the due penalty of their crime?"

Alexander, Earl of Ross, shuffled in his place. There was a cough, but no one said a word.

"So be it." James turned to William Keith. "My lord, you are to join Robert Lauder and take as many of our men as you think meet to pursue these malefactors. They are to be apprehended and returned to me for execution—forthwith."

As Keith bowed and withdrew, James said in a carefully even tone, " Sir Abbot, I was forced to interrupt the point you were making. My apologies. Now we may continue. You were about to say...?"

When the abbot gaped at him for a moment and stuttered out that he did not recall, James called for a vote. He was thankful he had never planned for this to be a truly productive parliament, because it was obvious that most were thinking of the fugitives and wondering if they would be caught.

It was near midnight when William Keith sent word that the three and a hundred of their followers had been tracked down. The fight had been hot for a few minutes, but all three were now captive. They had been heading for Lorne, where the Campbell could raise his spears by the thousand. James commanded that the three men were to be within the walls before daybreak to prevent any attempt to break them free.

It was a grim night in which he slept in snatches before waking to worry about the outcome of executions in a part of the realm where his writ ran so thin. But it had to be done, or he and the law would be held only in scorn.

As Catherine Douglas combed out the queen's long hair, he went to put a hand on her shoulder. "I hoped if I brought you, it would show that I wanted peace. And all I've succeeded in doing is putting you in danger." He took her hand. "Forgive me?"

Joan motioned Catherine away and squeezed James' hand. "Of course." She stood and brushed his lips with hers. "There is nothing to forgive. I'm Queen Consort and my place is with you."

"I'll not take such risks with you again. That I promise you."

She twined her arm through his and walked with him to the door. "I do not think I am in so much danger. I believe Ross would not be eager to kill a woman, and he brought his mother with him. The two of you were not so far apart as it might seem."

James had had an announcement proclaimed that the parliament would meet in the bailey yard of the castle. The three prisoners were led out, and William Keith read out the decision of the king in parliament and the sentence. One had tears streaming down his face, but the other two stared straight ahead, silent.

The keep's main door creaked as it opened. James flinched when he heard Joan's voice. "My lord king," she said in a soft, even voice. "I ask you to show mercy to these men. I do not question the rightness of their sentence, but mercy and clemency are right as well. By your love of me, I ask Your Grace to spare them."

James gripped is hands into fists, digging his nails into his palms, and drew a deep breath. He faced straight ahead because he could not stand to see the look on Joan's face. A moment stretched out unbearably in utter silence before he said, "No, it cannae be. I think of a certain verse I wrote:

To the tower perchance let us take this band,
For by Christ's Fate they earned their death."

There was a gasp from the crowd, so James could not tell if Joan made a sound. "To remit their sentences would destroy the authority of parliament and of the law. The authority of the very realm is at stake. I shall not grant Her Grace's request, however much I would want to. Proceed, My Lord Marischal."

James heard her footsteps as she walked away and the door to the keep close.

Keith continued, "The Court of Justiciary some years past convicted James Campbell of Lorne of the foul murder of Lord John of Islay, a relation of the present Lord of Islay. He has therefore forfeited his right to an honorable death and shall suffer a felon's death by hanging. Alexander Macruri and John MacArthur are hereby sentenced to death by beheading. God save the king!"

James Campbell struggled as he was dragged to a beam that projected from the parapet. He kicked and writhed as the noose was put about his neck and he was hoisted. Bile washed into James' mouth. He hadn't thought of the Scots King Henry had hanged in a very long time, but he made himself watch without flinching. Campbell continued to kick, his body shuddering for a full minute before he was still. Macruri prayed softly as he went to the block. John MacArthur glared for a moment at James and said, "I go to Heaven now, James Stewart. Will you be able to say the same?" A man-at-arms shoved him chest down onto the block.

Later, James slowly climbed the stairs to their chamber. Joan stood alone at the window, looking out at the distant mountains. "Your words were harsh," she said.

"Aye. My words and my actions. Forgive me. They were meant for the others, nae for you."

"I wish... I wish you could have granted my request. Mercy, just once, would seem to me to be a good thing." She turned, and her face was wet with tears.

"I could nae do it, love. If these Highlanders thought me weak, there would be no chance of governing the realm. I swore as solemn an oath as a man can take that I would never be too weak to govern. As my father was. It is..." He sighed. "It is more important to me than I can tell you."

She wiped her cheeks with the heel of her hand and nodded. "I did not truly think you could spare them. But I had to ask. And I hoped."

James went to her and pulled her gently against his chest. "If there is a next time, then I'll grant it. Whatever it may cost me." She leaned against him, and he rested his cheek against the top of her head, breathing in the scent of her rose water.

"Have you achieved what you wanted, James? Was it worth the cost?"

"I believe that I have. They know that the King's Grace

means what he says and that the law of the realm is nae to be defied. And the Earl of Ross now owes me a debt, for it was of his ilk whom Campbell had murdered, though he could nae exact justice for it. So, aye, the realm is strengthened this day."

Chapter Twenty

JUNE 23, 1429

Trumpets resounded and cut the air of the summer evening. Sendaris paled, jumped to his feet, and grabbed James' sword belt. James held up his hand and listened. There were shouts of "Mar! Mar!"

"Friends," James said. "I shan't need my sword yet. That will be the Earl of Mar."

James emerged from his tent into the translucent light of Lochaber. He gazed out over the sapphire ribbon of Loch Leven and the vast mountain vistas beyond and could almost forget he was here to kill his enemy, an enemy who had left a burning ruin behind them.

The earl clattered into camp and swung from the saddle; behind him were fifty knights and what looked like at least a thousand mounted men-at-arms strung out on the road. "Your Grace!" Mar called. The earl was even balder than the last time James saw him, but his short beard was still full. In his gilded armor, he strode toward James as hearty as ever. "You look well, Sire. Is it true Her Grace is with child again?" He handed his helm to a squire and wiped the sweat from the bare top of his head with a swipe.

"Three daughters in a row! Her Grace is praying daily for a son this time." He clapped Mar on the shoulder. "Come inside so we can talk."

"Aye, a son would solve many of our problems. Johne the Fat still has friends in the Highlands who would like to see him on your throne." Sendaris was pouring wine for them. "Have your scouts brought any word of that fool, Alexander MacDonald?" Mar loosened the clasp and tossed his cloak onto the bed.

"He left a clear enough trail after he burned Inverness. How far ahead of us, that they haven't yet brought back word." Ross had left the burgh of Inverness a smoldering ruin, although he hadn't been able to take the castle. James gave Mar a considering look. "Do you think it is a conspiracy with John that has the Earl of Ross rebelling?"

"I think he's merely a fool. What would burning Inverness do for putting that glutton John on the throne?"

"I confess that I rue that I didn't listen to you and accepted Ross into my peace. I'm a fool as well for trusting him."

Mar shrugged, took off his gauntlets, and took a cup from the squire. "You weren't reared by the Wolf of Badenoch."

"Nae, I was reared by the English, and they fed me on more scorn than Ross has seen in all his life," said James with a grim laugh. "He was offended because some of the nobles mocked his way of speaking. So he rebels. Damn him."

"How many men were you able to raise?"

"Three thousand. Most Douglas men and five hundred follow the Earl of Angus. Douglas is out with a scouting party now."

Mar drained his cup and tossed it to Sendaris. "Four thousand with mine will leave us a smaller force than Ross will have. So we must needs out-think him. That shouldn't be hard." Mar sat himself on a camp stool without awaiting permission, but James decided to ignore it. "He has raised a number of the smaller clans."

James tugged on his lower lip. He had never gone wrong taking Mar's advice on battle. The man was a savage, nearly as bad as his father, who was called the Wolf of Badenoch for good reason, but he knew as much about war as any man in Scotland, a good deal more than James did. "Douglas is scouting toward Loch Lochy. The scouts said their tracks led in that direction."

"And the scouts did nae know how many they followed? They should be able to tell that."

James lifted his cup and took a swallow. "Some thousands, but we have no way of knowing who has joined him. Who could have said our number before you joined us?"

Mar shrugged and took a fresh cup of wine from the squire.

"Do you have a plan for our strategy? If we are to out-think him?"

"Let us find them first. It's no use making plans in the dark. I learned that the hard way. If I had been wiser when I fought the Battle of Harlaw, I would have won instead of merely not losing. My mistake was splitting my army in three. It seemed like a good plan before I kent Ross's strength." He snorted a laugh through his nose. "Many good men and friends died because of it. Dinnae plan before you ken your enemy's strength. And his weakness."

"Whatever we do, we need to do it quickly. I can't afford for the realm to be weakened with Johne Stewart still lurking in Ireland." He smiled. "And I want to return to Edinburgh and my Queen."

"The queen thrives being with child again?"

"She is radiant, always her most beautiful when she's increasing." Last night he had dreamed that he took too long returning and she and the children had been stolen away. In his dream, he had used the Sword of State to slaughter every man in the castle in his rage. "The sooner we finish, Mar, the sooner I'll be back where I need to be."

There was the sound of hooves, the clatter of harness, and loud voices outwith the tent. John Cameron ducked his head inside. "Sire, Lord Douglas requests that you would join him. There is someone he says you should speak with."

James raised an eyebrow at so odd a request, but he went out to find the Earl of Douglas. Standing beside him was a tall, scrawny, stooping man in a rusty mail hauberk. Douglas called out, "Sire. We return with news." He led over his odd companion. "This is King James," he said as the man looked at the king with squinty, close-placed eyes. "This is Brian Cameron, Sire. He gave me news of the Earl of Ross that you need to hear."

Almost shyly, the man stepped forward and gave an awkward, bobbing bow. "The Ross, he has his men away yon to the north near Loch Lochy, and my chief, Donald Dhu, he be wi him."

"And you're betraying your own chief?" Mar barked in a horrified voice.

"I widnae betray him!" the man stuck out a stubborn chin. "He never wanted to follow the MacDonald, any road. He received word you needed men and raised our spears, but then the MacDonald came wi his whole force, so he joined them meantime. But I know he means to join you—" He wrinkled his forehead in puzzlement before he seemed to remember the right form of address. "Sire."

Mar spat. "You cannae trust these Highlanders, and I've told you so before, Your Grace. This Cameron and his chief would stab you in the back the first chance. And certes they'll betray you in battle."

The man paled in the face of Mar's rage, but he answered

anyway. "I never. I never betrayed no one, nor would I. Nor Donald Dhu."

James rubbed his palms together as he considered. "The question is do we trust Brian enough to send a message to Donald Dhu? He swore fealty to me at Stirling and behaved honorably at Inverness when he attended the parliament. So... Douglas, I heard Mar's advice. What say you?"

"You may strike me down if I'm lying," Brian insisted.

"That is easy for you say as we do not ken if you are lying," Douglas said thoughtfully. "If we send a message to the Cameron and he betrays us, we not only give up any chance of a surprise but give Ross a chance to attack us. But Ross must have a larger force; I expect he will have twice our numbers. I think..." He looked a long time at the man. "I think we must take the risk."

"My lord... Sire..." Brian stuttered. "There is something else that would be worth knowing. The Ross summoned the Mackintosh of Clan Chattan from Badenoch. He arrived the day. He has no love for the earl, and he and Donald Dhu both are loyal men if you gie them a chance."

"So...both Clan Cameron and Clan Chattan." He tilted his head, examining the man's face, trying to decide if this was worth a huge risk. "How many men does Donald Dhu Cameron have at his back?"

The man scratched the back of his neck. "I have nae numbers that big. Every fighting man of our clan is wi him."

Mar made a sound in his throat as though he were beginning to consider the idea. "Probably a thousand from what I know of the Camerons. A few more caterans would follow Mackintosh. But if Clan Chattan has arrived, why has Ross's army not moved?" He glared, hard faced, at the Cameron.

"They arrived the day wearied from the long trek. The earl is nae going to discuss his plans wi the likes of me, but I suppose he wanted them to rest for the next march."

Mar's grunt was reluctantly in agreement that this made sense.

For another minute, James fingered his short beard. "I find him convincing. We will take the chance. But we have little time, so we must not delay."

With James harrying them, they broke camp within the hour. Cameron and Douglas's scouts led them first up the first ridge to the east and then north, squelching through bogs and clambering through hollows, as they skirted Ben Nevis, forced to lead their horses most of the time. It was ten long and weary miles of slogging, dripping sweat, and swatting midges that plagued them. But there was no time to lose if they were to reach the army of the Earl of Ross in time to take advantage of their plan.

When they reached the edge of the emerald-green Glen Nevis, Mar stated that with their numbers, if they went closer, the enemy would certainly hear their approach, so the Cameron and two of Mar's men went ahead, Brian Cameron with orders to return to his Clan Chief to warn him of their approach. The short time stretched like an eternity, but the scouts returned with word that Ross's army was still camped with no sign of moving and indeed at least twice the number of their own.

With the earls of Douglas, Mar, and Angus and Sir David Douglas of Whittinghame, James made his way to the crest of the ridge and, on his belly, peered over at the army below. It was chaos, with hundreds of campfires, men lounging and drinking, some bent over their fires cooking their dinner. The paths between the campfires were brown earth, torn by hoof and boot. Horses were picketed on the edge of the camp, but others were tied at the scattered tents. Cattle roamed the edge of the glen, booty from ravaged villages and valleys. A great pavilion stood at one side with a pole that flew the black galley, sails furled, on white that was the banner of the chief of Clan MacDonald, the Lord of the Isles and Earl of Ross. James grunted in satisfaction; in one corner of the camp there was quiet bustle as horses were led from the picket and caterans gathered near two small pavilions, but by no means was this a camp expecting an attack.

James scooted a short way down the slope, out of sight. He nodded to Mar to give the orders. James was not fool enough to think he was a better tactician than the earl.

"We need to reach our positions as far as we can from the camp. Move quickly and quietly. Whittinghame, you take your men to the right flank. Angus to the left. Every banner and pennon should be flown to make our force appear as large as we may. We'll watch for smoke to signal you're in position. Once we top the ridge so the king's banner is shown, ride out and signal. If Cameron and Chattan do as they should..." He grimaced. "If they do as they should, then we'll charge. If they fail us, we'll know soon enough, and it will be a fight for our lives."

Since this was the third time Mar had gone over the battle plan, the two men asked no questions. They ran hunched down the slope. While they waited, James moved the few thousand horsemen into position out of sight at the base of the ridge. It was a long wait as the sun sank until was a mere hand's width above the horizon. At last, a narrow stream of smoke wafted from the flanks.

James climbed into the saddle, drew his sword and waved it overhead to signal the trumpeters. Scrymgeour lifted the huge royal banner on its pole. Up went the banner of Douglas with its stars and crowned heart and the blue and white checked banner with bars sinister for Mar and a dozen pennons for the lesser lords and knights.

Haroooo The trumpets blared out a challenge. James touched his heels to his horse's flanks. At a fast walk, they rode up the slope and pulled up when they topped the ridge.

Below them, the camp was chaos, men running for horses, shouting, grabbing pikes and Lochaber axes. James raised his sword over his head once more and waved it. Again the trumpets rang out and seemed to echo off the mountains.

On both sides, from the flanks men burst out from the trees and galloped toward the camp to pull up a short distance away, shouting, "A Cameron! A Cameron!" and "Mackintosh!"

Within the camp, Donald Dhu and his clansmen leapt onto their waiting horses, the foot soldiers grabbed up their axes, and they ran, joining in the shout and adding ululating shouts in Gaelic and bloodcurdling shrieks. Nearby, Mackintosh had turned his rearing mount and rallied his men. Like a surging wave, they ran toward the flanks, screaming war cries and howling as they went.

Alexander of Ross was standing in front of his pavilion, cursing and shouting. When a squire ran up with a horse, he threw himself into the saddle. "To me!" James heard him screaming over the pandemonium around him. "To me!"

"Attack!" James shouted and put his spurs to his horse. Before them, Alexander Stewart, Earl of Ross, turned his horse's head and fled. The Highlanders were reeling from the shock of the attack and of two clans leaving the field. In only the time it took to take a breath, the battle was a rout. Every many who could reach a horse flung himself upon it and rode desperately after the earl. The caterans threw down their weapons, or some ran, only to be cut down.

Mar cut down a cateran who was fool enough to run at him. A thrown axe rattled on James' shield. James wheeled and raced after the thrower. When the man turned to run, he fell and James rode over him, wheeled again and rode for Ross's tent. He slashed the ropes and it collapsed in a heap. Riderless horses neighed and bolted, dodging the fleeing men.

The stolen cattle stampeded and ran pell-mell, knocking down anyone in their path.

James pulled up and slowly circled his mount. There was no one to fight. The battle, such as it was, was over. James snorted, sheathed his sword, and threw back his head as laugher rolled out of him in waves.

Mar trotted up and shook his head. "You were right, Sire. I confess it. Now we must pursue them. See that they dinnae rally! Smite them whilst we may."

"Aye, no doubt you're right." James breathed another faint chuckle through his nose. "Take your own men and smite any enemies you can find, but I suspect these Highlanders may be good at fleeing through their own bogs."

James looked around. A golden sunset spread across the western sky and purple shadows were creeping across the wide glen. A fine night was upon them, and the utter humiliation of Alexander of Islay felt even better than killing him.

Chapter Twenty-One
AUGUST 28, 1429

In his finest robes, Bishop Wardlaw, still sturdier than one would think a man of his age could be, was conducting the Mass. The church of Holyrood Abbey was filled with the pleasant scent of beeswax candles and frankincense, and a hint of the rose scent that Joan wore as she sat in a throne beside him added a fillip to his pleasure in their place before the high altar.

James couldn't help the pleased smirk even in the midst of a celebration of the mass. It had taken two years, two frustrating years, but at least the Pope had needed support from James enough to give in to his insistence. John Cameron was now Bishop of Glasgow and assisting Wardlaw in the Mass. At last, only yesterday, James had officially named him Chancellor of Scotland and Keeper of the Great Seal.

He looked out over the crowded church filled with his court in their finery. The realm was at peace, and if Alexander, Earl of Ross, had escaped the campaign of the previous summer, that was a problem that did not seem very serious at the moment. Rarely had he felt so at peace with himself and the world. Bishop Wardlaw was intoning a prayer: *Misereàtur nostri omnìpotens Deus et, dimìssis peccàtis nostris, perdùcat nos ad vitam aetèrnam.* James let the sounds and the scents wash over him.

Suddenly there was an uproar outwith the church. A guard shouted, and the door was flung open in an unpleasant reminder of the parliament at Inverness. James started upright and put a hand out to Joan, laying it on her arm.

A man strode in, a guard trailing behind and protesting. "My lord! You cannae go in dressed so!"

James stood. Alexander of Ross stood stock still, dressed only in a loose shirt, legs and feet bare, but with a sword in his hand. Joan made a gasping sound and James stepped in front of her. But the sword in Ross's hand was reversed, and he held it—very carefully—by the point. James raised an eyebrow as he motioned the guard back. Another trick by the Earl of Ross, but James thought he would let it play itself out. Joan stood close behind him and grasped his arm in both hands.

All around the church, men were rising to their feet. Murmurs and whispers went through the crowd, but no one wore a sword to church. But Ross simply strode up the central aisle, looking neither right nor left, keeping his gaze humbly down on James' feet. James wanted to laugh. He would never believe humility in the Lord of the Isles. But when he reached James, Ross dropped to both knees and offered the sword, hilt first.

"I beg Your Grace to admit me to your peace," he said, his voice was shaking. A good act, James mused. "I confess my faults and my crimes and submit myself to your justice. I beg your royal mercy, Sire."

A rustling of whispers went through the church as everyone craned to see this strange and unexpected spectacle at the same time a sigh of relief sounded as well. James stared at the man kneeling at his feet. If he had ever thought Ross was stupid, this proved him wrong—unless someone had suggested this stratagem to him. James looked from Ross to Joan. A slight smile curved her lips.

"You beg mercy after the crimes you have committed.?" James shook his head. "I do beg your compassion and pity. I place my person in your hands, my king. In token thereof, I beg that you take my sword."

He extended it and James looked at it with a grimace of distaste. This was the veriest playacting, all deceit with no honesty in it. By surrendering in a church where he could not be seized, was in fact in sanctuary, he had managed to put James in a difficult position. His wife knew him well. "I pardoned you once, even took you into my household. Yet you burned the burgh of Inverness, killed, stole, and ravaged the north of the realm. Defied my justice. Raised your hand against me. Why should I touch your sword, blemished as it is with sin and crime?"

Near the rear of the church, the Earl of Atholl stood up. "Your Grace, surely in the church before the very altar, mercy should be given even to a criminal. Consider, nephew, that all of us require forgiveness in this life. I beg that you offer it to Alexander MacDonald."

James stared at his uncle. They had never become close, but since his return, the man had always been quietly loyal. And James owed him consideration for bringing word of the Albany rebellion to him. He turned his head to look at Joan, and clasping his hand in both of hers, she slowly knelt at his feet. "I add my plea, Your Grace. By your love of me, please offer him mercy. He admits his faults and his crimes. Can you not spare his life?"

He tugged at her. "Do not grovel, love. It is not seemly. Since you ask it of me." He sighed slightly. "I grant your request." He reached out and reluctantly grasped the hilt of the sword that Ross still extended to him. "The sentence of death passed by the parliament on Alexander MacDonald is remitted. All of his titles and estates are hereby forfeit." James looked around the church until he spotted the Earl of Angus. "My lord Earl, take this man into your custody and confine him in your Castle of Tantallon until I require him of you. I bid you hold him most securely."

James blew out a long breath. But the Earl of Atholl was walking up the center aisle and said, "I would make another request of you, Your Grace. Sir Robert Graham awaits without also to throw himself on your royal mercy. I beg you consider extending what you offered to Alexander MacDonald to him. I kent him as a lad; his father was a friend. If you feel you owe me some consideration, give him your compassion and receive him into your peace."

James sank down onto his throne and looked at his beautiful wife. She smiled and shrugged a little. Why not? Graham can do me no harm, James thought. "I grant your plea, uncle."

Chapter Twenty-Two

FEBRUARY 1430

James reflectively eyed Henry Beaufort, now a cardinal and still Chancellor of England. The years had changed him little. He was still the greedy Sassenach he had always been, and James had no reason to trust him more than he had in those days of imprisonment in England, which was why they were meeting now in Coldingham Priory a bit north of Berwick-upon-Tweed. James certainly did not trust either Beaufort or the English enough to set foot in that kingdom.

That Beaufort had agreed to a council within Scotland, braving February chill and rains, and had travelled so far meant that he wanted something. The man did nothing that was not to his own benefit. Light from the blazing fire on the hearth in the Prior's study glittered on the rich brocade of Beaufort's gown, the gold of fittings of his belt, and the gems in the rings on his fingers as he gave James his blessing.

Even with the fire, there was a moist chill in the air that matched the cool calculation of Beaufort's greeting. Henry Percy's greeting had been warmer, though the strain of disputes over the truce had put a chill in even their old friendship. "Your Grace," Percy exclaimed and gave his braying laugh. "Strange to give you that title after all these years." The years had not been particularly kind to Percy. The man's girth had grown to match his height and his short beard did nothing to hide his double chin and the sag of his jowls, yet he was only a few years older than James himself.

But Percy was a friend from his childhood and an envoy in his realm, so James said, "Henry, it is fine to see you looking so well."

Lord John Scrope, a short wiry man, his hair lightly salted with white, made a deep bow. "It is an honor, Your Grace."

James took the prior's chair comfortably placed near the fire, which earned a glare from the sullen-faced Beaufort. After a servant had poured their wine and retired, James gave Beaufort a sly smile and said, "It is indeed fine to see old friends from my days in England and France. Mayhap you've visited with Duke Philip of Burgundy. He and I were comrades in arms in those days." He smiled broadly at Beaufort. The rumors had been rife for months that in spite of having turned the Maid of Orleans over to the English, Philip was deep in negotiations for making peace with Charles and returning to the French side.

Beaufort sputtered. "Duke Philip is a good friend to the English as always, and thanks to him we'll soon be rid of that witch, that so called Maid of Orleans! Once that is done and her evil influence destroyed, we shall have the Dauphin on the run once more."

James sipped his wine and mused that perhaps poking at Beaufort was not wise since they were to negotiate, but he gently sat down his cup and said, "Dauphin? I must have been misinformed by my envoys to France, who told me that Charles was at Reims last year."

"His crowning meant nothing," Beaufort said stiffly. "I would remind Your Grace that the crowned King of France is Henry Plantagenet."

"She enchanted him; otherwise he never would have had the courage to put the crown on his head," Percy put in.

"Ah. And yet he did so. Removing a crown once it's placed is not always an easy matter."

"Merest folly," Beaufort said. "There have been setbacks this last year. I admit as much, but that will not last. I assure you that the Duke of Bedford will soon put things to right."

"Mayhap, but I suspect the...attrition in your war with France may be why you found reason to visit me here in Coldingham."

"Not at all, Your Grace," Beaufort protested. "I am charged with expressing the loving regard of our liege lord King Henry and to convey all of our congratulations on the birth of your two sons. What a great gift of the Good God, two sons born to you in one day."

"My thanks." James nodded. In fact, it was a sore point which he certainly would not share with the oily Beaufort. Joan was worried almost to death over the sickly elder of their twin boys, and James feared that Alexander might not survive. Every day the child weakened yet more. There seemed to be some weakness in his breathing that no physician could cure. Yet the younger, James, was a strong, lusty babe. He begrudged being from Joan's side for even long enough for this meeting, for she would most surely need him if Alexander should die as he dreaded. He continued smoothly with what was no doubt a false-looking smile, "But I have no doubt so illustrious ambassadors as the Cardinal Beaufort and the Earl of Northumberland did not journey so far to merely convey congratulations that could have been sent in letters."

"I assure you the wishes are most sincere, although we would bring up a private matter in addition to expressing our deep love for Your Grace." Beaufort looked in his cup and

135

swirled the dark wine. "The Privy Council bade me to bring up the marriage of our liege lord, King Henry."

James steepled his fingers beneath his chin. He suspected that the Privy Council bade whatever Henry Beaufort told it to.

"His Grace approaches a marriageable age, and so we are seeking an appropriate bride, one of a royal house. The Privy Council believes that The Lady Margaret would make an excellent queen for our young king. They are close in age. Her mother is near to the royal house but not so close in consanguinity that the Pope would deny dispensation for the marriage."

James smiled mildly. He would force Beaufort to say the truth of the matter. "I have three daughters. I am sure that we could consider promising one of them to the King of England."

"Exactly what we have come to consider," Beaufort said looking satisfied. "The eldest princess, of course."

James leaned back in his chair. "Your Reverence, I regret to tell you that my eldest daughter is already promised to young Louis, Dauphin of France. But I would be happy to discuss one of my other daughters."

Scrope leaned forward eagerly. "They have no formal betrothal. It is only a promise, so it could be undone as we are suggesting."

"I am not in the habit of undoing my promises," James said.

"Sometimes one must do what is best for the realm even if it means doing something...regrettable. You must agree that a marriage to the King of England would be better for all than a marriage to this false-Dauphin, for he is not even truly that."

"And yet he might be soon, for your conquest of France is not looking certain, my lords. Not certain at all."

"We have had no more than setbacks," Percy put in. "We still have Paris and will soon regain what has been lost."

Lord Scrope was nodding vigorously. "Exactly."

"And you would seek to guarantee this regaining of what was lost by preventing a resumption of Scotland's Auld Alliance with France. And what do you propose that the Scots would receive for this?" James looked from one of the Englishmen to another and slowly nodded. "Aye, there we have it, then. Only the daughter who is promised to the Dauphin is to be considered. That is exactly what I suspected. You have no desire for a Scottish princess to marry your king, but only to deny a French alliance to the Scots." He raised an eyebrow. "And where would your armies turn if you did indeed batter the French into submission, My Lords? How long would a peace treaty keep you from turning your eyes upon Scotland?"

"No, Your Grace," said Beaufort, indignantly. "How can you think we would break such a treaty?"

"As you broke the sea truce when I was taken prisoner to be held for eighteen years?" James stood, which forced the other three men to stand as well. "I do not break my word, my lords. My daughter is promised to the Dauphin. And as for continuing the truce, I shall take it up with my parliament."

Chapter Twenty-Three

The parliament was once again being held in the refectory of Blackfriars Monastery in Perth. James looked with some satisfaction at the gathering, for the Highland Lairds were well represented, including Alexander MacDonald, whom he had released from imprisonment and returned to his grace the year before, though he had not returned the earldom of Ross to him. In spite of occasional outbreaks of violence in the Highlands, James was convinced he had brought most into his peace. The burghers were well represented and most of the Lowland lords were present. He took his place on the throne, and John Cameron, for some time now the chancellor, banged his gavel and announced that they would consider the proposal of renewing the Auld Alliance with France.

Since his son David's death in England, the Earl of Atholl had aged almost beyond recognition. His face was gaunt, and his hands shook as he stood to speak. "Your Grace, I must tell you that an alliance with France is utter folly. Never when we have had an alliance with them have they defended Scotland, but always our blood has been poured out on their soil to defend them. Nor is their King Charles likely in the end to defeat the English. And once they are defeated and we've made an enemy to the south, what are we to do?"

There were some murmurs of agreement in the refectory, and Atholl seemed satisfied when he took his seat. Cameron recognized MacDonald, who argued in favor of seeking a permanent peace treaty with England. Not being forced to fight English pirates at sea would be an advantage for the Islemen, who depended much on their galleys and sea trade.

The Bishop of Argyll rose, shaking his head. "Folly? Is it folly to prefer to fight our enemies in France rather than on our own soil? I say it would be folly to allow the English to conquer France, for if they did, you may be sure their next prize would be Scotland. I have no great love for the French, but that is not the root of the Auld Alliance. France and Scotland need each other. We need each other no less now than we have in the past. His Grace has agreed to a five-year renewal of the Border truce. We need no more than that. And while that is in place we must succor the French if Scotland itself is to survive."

At the rear of the refectory, Sir Robert Graham leapt to his feet and waved to the chancellor. Before he was even given leave, he was shouting, "My Lords, you are being deceived. Lied to by traitors, men greedy for our lands. Churchmen in the pay of the French and a King who betrays—"

The uproar drowned out his voice. Cameron banged his gavel. Everywhere men were shouting. Mar jumped to his feet and was roaring curses at the man. "Silence!" Cameron shouted. "In the name of the king! Silence!" He banged his gavel again. When the hall had quieted, although there was still a buzz of whispers, Cameron asked Mar to take his seat. The earl did so with obvious reluctance.

"Sir Robert, you have the right to speak in this parliament, but not to speak slander and calumnies. That is to cease forthwith."

Graham sneered. "Aye, I see this is the freedom of speech of the parliament we were promised by this...this...king. This tyrant! Speak what his chancellor tells you or have your lands stolen from you."

Cameron hammered the gavel, his face crimson with fury. "For the last time! Keep a civil tongue!"

"Wait!" James held up a hand. "My Lord Chancellor, as Sir Robert has said I have declared freedom of speech in the parliament. I would hear what he has to say. He has allegations to lay so let him lay them."

Cameron bowed to the king before he turned back to the parliament. "You heard the king. Of his mercy, you may speak. I say the word traitor comes strangely from a man convicted of treason, but name your traitors then, if you can."

Graham's face twisted into a snarl, a mask of hatred. "The king! I name the king a traitor and tyrant. And you, John Cameron, as his tool. Both of you have sold us to the French and stolen our lands and our rights. Turned Scottish barons into lapdogs. You and your master are the traitors in Scotland!"

Cameron jumped from his chair, his face a chalky white, and all around there was a pandemonium of shouts, but none of it was a match for the screech of hatred from Robert Graham.

He thrust a finger at James. "There!" he screamed. "There is the tyrant! James Stewart! Thief! Murderer! Traitor!" Graham was gasping for air after his outburst.

Mar was once more on his feet shouting, "Seize him! This is madness!"

Sir William Hay, the High Constable, was already signaling for guards who had been to frozen by shock to do more than gape. Two guards rushed to seize Graham, who seemed stunned by his own outbursts. He hung between them unresisting.

"Silence," James said in a quiet voice. "High Constable, escort Sir Robert from the chamber."

There were gasps and then shouts of "Treason!" and "Behead him!" and "Put him to death!" from all around the chamber.

The Earl of Atholl stood and said, "Your Grace, you promised him freedom of speech, so I trust you are not going to arrest him. It must be brain fever or some temporary madness. I am sure he did not mean what he said."

James rose to his feet. "You are right, uncle. It was lèse-majesté, but I do not break my promises." He nodded to the High Constable. "Escort him from the monastery and he may go where he wills, but he shall not be allowed to return to parliament."

Graham was led out, unresisting, but no shouting or beating of the gavel quieted the uproar that followed, so James called for a vote on the maintaining the alliance with France. It was some relief to him when it passed. Atholl stomped away, scowling and grumbling under his breath.

James breathed a sigh of relief and went to spend an hour of peace with Joan and the children.

Chapter Twenty-Four

When Wardlaw stepped through the door, James, writing, put down his quill and said, "Your Reverence. Is it still raining? I hope your journey was nae too uncomfortable." He rose and said to a hovering servant, "Where is the wine? The bishop is weary. What? No sweetcakes?" He sighed. "Must I have the queen present to be well served?"

Then the room was bustling. Food and wine were carried in, the fire stirred. A page took the primate's wet cloak with a murmured apology. The servants slipped away, the door was closed, and James waved his guest to a seat and himself brought the bishop a goblet of sweet, rich malmsey.

"As for Your Grace's business with the Holy See..."

"I am listening." James sat down and regarded the bishop, waiting.

Wardlaw was dressed in blackish-purple robes and fine white lace, though they were limp from the damp. His jowls hung loose and his hands were spotted with age, but he still had a hawk's gaze that stabbed when he looked James' way. He set the wine aside and sighed. "I was afeart it would come to this, Sire. From the first when you proposed the laws against the Church, I warned you. And then, in spite of the appeals of the Holy Father, you refused to send a delegate to the Congress of Arras." Wardlaw shook his head sadly, his jowls swinging. "You must return to obedience, Your Grace, or he will be forced to harsher action."

"Continue, Reverence," James said. "Indeed, I wait to be instructed as a good son of the Church."

The light through the windows was dim, and rain splattered against the glass of the window.

"In the next parliament, you must repeal the laws that harm the rights of the Church. I would say that you should call a parliament now, but if I write to him that you swore to me that you will act in the next one, I believe the Pope will hold his anger."

James stared at his desk, at the poem he had half written. He looked up. A draft from beneath the side door made the candles bend and then they straightened. "So if I change the laws and give the Holy See more power in Scotland, he will be satisfied."

"And he would have you give aid to the French."

A log split in the fireplace with a loud snap; James rose and prodded it with the poker. He stood for a few moments, twisting the rings on his fingers and thinking. "I give you my word that I will think deeply on your advice." He turned back to the bishop. "Now you've had a long journey. Rest. We will speak further another time."

Wardlaw opened his mouth to protest, but James took him gently by the arm and showed him to the door. He jested, "Mayhap you would have a word with God so that your king and his Court could have a surcease of rain and ride out to the hunt instead of hunkering inside; it would clear his mind to consider what you have said."

Wardlaw sketched a blessing as James closed the door.

There was a sound of the side door and a footstep. "What do you think?" James asked.

"You will nae like it."

"All the more reason to hear."

"I think that he has gone over to the Pope, even acts as his spy."

James nodded slowly and crossed to the table to pour himself another goblet of wine. "I fear you may be right. Which means that we must see to our own support. We must not be at war with the Holy See, so how best to achieve that?"

"Without giving up the laws limiting the Pope's power, you mean. I think we must give up something, but he also wants you to give aid to the French. If you do that, it will lessen the price."

James sank into his chair and motioned Cameron to assume Wardlaw's place. "I mean to do that any road, though I shall nae send them an army. Since the Duke of Burgundy has abandoned the English and gone over to Charles, it is safe for Margaret to marry the Dauphin, though I shall not rush her departure."

"It will be late for this year's sailing season, certes it will be by the time a French fleet arrives. An easy excuse for more delay, but we must persuade the Pope to send a nuncio, one who can be convinced that you are in the right. Or persuade the cardinals who will persuade the Pope, and what will persuade them is a bag of gold."

"So when I send you to Rome, it must be with a great deal of ready coin," James said, smiling wryly. "Who will you induce them to send as a nuncio?"

"Anthony Altani, Bishop of Urbino, seemed to me a most reasonable man when I was last in Rome. He is, shall we say, less the Pope's man than the Pope believes him to be, but I fear Wardlaw's reports of me will have been unfavorable. Do not expect His Holiness will allow me to return soon."

"Ah, well," James said, "I would there were another way. You must travel well prepared for a long stay."

Chapter Twenty-Five

FEBRUARY 1436

In her piping, nine-year-old's voice, Margaret read:
"For he would rather have at his beddes head
Twenty bookes, clothed in black or red,
Of Aristotle, and his..." She made an uncertain hum. "And his..."

Margaret leaned an elbow on the table, covered by a silk carpet, and bit her lip as she puzzled over the next word. James waited whilst she worked it out, tempted to touch the tumble of golden curls down her back, so like her mother's. But when she looked up at him and frowned, he saw a great deal of himself in her long, narrow Stewart nose and large eyes. She was the most like him of all their brood in looks and in her love of books and poetry, and he loved her fiercely for it.

The fire on the hearth crackled pleasantly into the chamber's silence.

"It's a very big word. I dinnae know it, Papa."

"And his philosophie." James smiled at the slight roll of her eyes at the unfamiliar word. The thought of sending her away gave him tightness in his chest.

"We should join our guests, Your Grace," Joan said from the doorway. James looked over his shoulder to give a puzzled look and realized she was dressed for the evening's feast with a heart-shaped, veiled headdress and belted, fur-lined blue velvet gown open at the front to display the silk chemise beneath.

Behind her, the nurse led four-year-old James by the hand. Joan was rarely so formal en famille. But she was right for an ambassador from the French king was with them for the aguillanneuf festivities to see in the New Year. He checked his new doublet, crimson silk with the sleeves slashed to show the green satin lining. He took Joan's arm and escorted her to the great hall, followed by Margaret who muttered under her breath at having to walk with her brother.

The heralds blew their trumpets to signal their entrance into the hall, hung with evergreens that scented the air. It was a blaze of light from colored lanterns and set for feasting. All was ease and laughter amongst eddies of nobles in silk, satin, and velvet. Minstrels played from the gallery as all in the crowded room swept the four of them deep bows and curtsies. James led Joan around to receive the expected courtesies.

He watched Margaret tell the Earl of Douglas that she was pleased to see him once more at court, compliment Eupheme Graham on her gown although it clashed badly with her pale complexion, and question the French ambassador, Regnault Girard, whether the Dauphin was as gallant as rumor stated. She will do well at the French court, he thought. The Earl of Mar kissed her hand, but James was shocked at his appearance. His face was drawn beneath hair gone gray, and he had lost all the flesh from his frame. He stumbled slightly as he bowed over Joan's hand. Yet when Margaret praised all she had heard of his valor in battle, he beamed. She will make a good queen for the French, but Sweet Mary let them learn to love her as we do. Rumor said the Dauphin quarreled often with his father, but the boy had his duty as they all did. James' duty was giving up his daughter.

Girard's spotty son, Sir Joachim, swaggered up to them in a cloth-of-gold doublet with black satin sleeves and said, "You have never seen anything so fine as our ship that will take you to France. The plates are all of gold and it carries only the finest wine." He shrugged. "It is called the Marie of Scotland though there is nothing of Scotland about it."

"What a kindness to provide such a fine ship," said Margaret, "but it is nae my place to discuss my departure until His Grace permits it."

The severe-looking Regnault Girard moved in quickly and cut off his son's sneering reply. "I am desolate." He raised an eyebrow at Joachim. "My son meant no disrespect, I assure you, Your Grace."

Prince James had scrunched up his face and was sticking his tongue out as far as it would go at his sister. She tilted her head towards her father and rolled her eyes. Joan grasped the prince's hand with a shake of her head.

"The saints forfend that I take offence." James smiled amiably. If the young knight's bad manners put his father at a disadvantage in the negotiations tomorrow, he wouldn't complain too harshly. Under no circumstances would he allow Margaret to travel by sea in such in the winter, and he would expect a larger convoy of ships for her protection than they had so far offered.

"If you will excuse us, Sir Regnault, it is time for The Lady Margaret to see her brother to his nurse."

Prince James glowered up at his mother. "I want a sweetie." He blinked hard obviously trying to manage a tear. "You said."

"Ah, it is true, all sons can be difficult, I daresay, Your Grace," the ambassador said with a sympathetic look.

James gave his son a forbidding stare. "Enough. You may have your sweetie with your nurse, but only if you mend your manners. Tell your lady sister you are sorry."

The prince kicked the rug but muttered he was sorry as Joan signaled to a page to begin the seating. Margaret swept a very mature curtsey to the ambassador and his son before she led her brother, dragging his feet, toward the door. The guests milled as pages sorted them out and showed them to their proper places on the benches.

James held out his arm for Joan's hand, and they strolled to their places on the dais in the seats of honor beneath a great lion rampant banner, draped for the occasion in swaths of evergreen and mistletoe. "To the ambassador of our good friends the French!" James proclaimed when the Bishop of Moray had finished the blessing. The page filled his goblet with the rich red Burgundy wine that had been one of the ambassador's gifts to the queen.

If the cries of "To the ambassador!" were less than enthusiastic, James knew it was because too many Scots had died fighting in France. Now the French wanted him for the first time in his reign to send more troops, but even so, hundreds of goblets were lifted and the New Year's feast began. James lifted his cup to the ambassador who sat two places from the queen, higher than his rank normally would have allowed, but the ambassador could hardly be slighted. Beside her the Earl of Mar shakily rose to salute the ambassador as well.

The first dish was frumenty of barley and venison, served in silver bowls. James patted his stomach. Some people said he was getting fat, but his stomach was only a bit fuller than when he returned home. He had eaten lightly as was right during the Nativity fasting, so he quickly finished the dish.

As the pages set out plates of salmon poached in ale, Mar began coughing. He sucked down a gasp of breath with a harsh rasp, and Regnault Girard pounded him on the back.

Joan was asking the earl if he was well. James signaled for the page to refill the earl's wine cup.

"I cannae..." Mar clutched his chest. "I canne breath..." he wheezed. Grasping his cup in a shaking hand, he took a swallow and hacked again. He shoved his chair back, his face a milky white.

Joan looked at him worriedly. "My lord?"

"Something...something is squeezing..." He grasped the edge of the table, slid to his knees, and then sank onto the floor.

"Call my physician!" James commanded. The Earl of Douglas rushed up, pushing Regnault Girard aside, to rip open the collar of Mar's doublet.

"Hurts..." Mar whispered.

Douglas lifted him and put a wine cup to his lips, but the wine dribbled out of the man's slack mouth. He is dying, James realized. James' physician bustled in, ordering everyone back as men shouted useless advice. All the guests were on their feet, pushing each other for a better view of what was happening. Mar's eyes met James'. He had never before seen the man look afraid, and he knew he was losing his best ally. Then he colored with shame and whispered, "Réquiem ætérnam dona ei, Dómine."

The bishop lifted his crucifix from around his neck and held it before the eyes of the stricken earl.

Chapter Twenty-Six
JUNE 1436

James paced his council chamber of Linlithgow Palace, a letter crushed in his hand. Parting with Margaret had been one of the most painful things James had ever had to do. The French fleet that came for her was large and richly provisioned. He sent a goodly household of Scots of good family under the care of the Earl of Orkney with her and many of her beloved books. He had escorted her onto the ship himself and kissed her farewell. But none of it was a salve for the grief of his losing his oldest child. At eleven, she looked so much like her mother, but she was like him. He felt closer to her than to any of his other children, as much as he loved them all.

An English fleet had been sent to intercept her. How dare they? The damned English had attacked her squadron. Only luck had allowed them to escape a sea battle. And there was yet a year left in the truce at land and sea. To try to capture her, endanger her life, it was beyond words. He slammed his fists down on the council table, wishing it were an English face. Any English face.

There was a soft, hesitant knock on the door before John

Cameron opened it. "Your Grace, I'm sorry, but there is news from the Border."

James flung himself down in a chair and scrubbed his face with his hands. From the look on his chancellor's face, this could not be good news. "Tell me."

"The English crossed Tweed near Wark in force. The Warden sent word that he does not have the men to fight them. They're crossing the Merse, burning and pillaging as they go."

James narrowed his gaze at Cameron. "The Earl of Angus is the nearest of the Douglases. Send word to him by the fastest courier. He must raise the largest force he can within three days and march south. Put a stop to the English raid." Cameron started to bow but James said, "Wait. It is time that the English learn that truce breaking is not to be tolerated. Once that is done, return; we shall raise me an army. I'll lead it to take back Roxburgh."

Raising an army was a matter of weeks, but by the end of July, a large army was camped before the towering spires of Kelso Abbey hard by Roxburgh Castle. There was good reason Roxburgh had remained in English hands when every other castle had been taken back. It was on an isthmus approachable by only a narrow strip, had walls as high and thick as any castle in Scotland, was near the border so it was easily reinforced, and its burgh was immediately under its walls, which meant bombardment would cause a huge loss of Scottish lives. So James knew they were in for a long siege, which he had had enough experience in whilst in France. So he sent a portion of his force down Tweed to besiege Berwick to prevent reinforcement from there, and the rest he used to cut off Roxburgh Castle.

The castle was out of cannon range from the far river-banks, and a direct assault up the narrow isthmus—which was ditched and moated under a line of flanking towers—would be a death trap. That left only mining or a prolonged siege to starve out the defenders. After long thought, James decided to try both.

Access to the isthmus was cut off by barriers and patrols sent out to be sure supplies did not reach them by boat. By night he sent miners and sappers to undermine the towers. Thus the pattern of the siege developed. By day, James allowed anything to keep his troops occupied. But it would be a matter of months, perhaps as many as six. He renewed his love of wrestling with matches, though he'd broadened with age so decided he was more fit to supervise. He held tourneys and archery contests and had jugglers and minstrels sent—anything to keep his troops out of trouble, because if they were bored, they'd be as like to kill each other as the English.

He was in the abbot's office going over the progress of the sappers with one of the engineers when there was a commotion outwith the doors and shouting that riders were arriving. James hurried out to see a train of fifty men-at-arms led by the queen. He lifted her from her horse, but before he could question her, she said, "Important news, Sire, that I must give you privily."

She ran her hands up and down her arms as though she was chilled in the heat of the summer's day. With the door closed behind them, she whirled and said, "Thomas Myrton brought me...such frightening word, love. I came to you myself because I have no way of knowing who to trust. He has word of a plot. A plot to kill you and seize the throne. He was brought letters intercepted that say some of your army will turn on you when you are attacked. They are to time it with an attack of galleys from the Clyde."

"Thomas Myrton said this?" James looked away, blinking and trying to make sense of what she was saying. "I'd trust him with my life, but it makes no sense. Never has my reign been more secure. I have an army raised to my banner. The

Albanys are dead or fled from the realm. My other enemies put to flight."

"But not all, James. Not all. What of Sir Robert Graham? He is not loyal, and you know he is not the only one who resists your new laws. Who feels you've seized more than you should."

"Our Lady forfend!" James rubbed his mouth. "Who could seize the throne? John the Fat is dead. Young James is healthy and my heir even if they managed to kill me."

"Thomas Myrton thinks it has to be your uncle. The Earl of Atholl. Only you and James are between him and the throne."

James gaped at her, shaking his head.

"The plot as Myrton heard it is that they will pronounce you wrongfully crowned...claim that you and your father are of a bastard line."

"That's an old tale that no one takes seriously." James began to pace anxiously around the room. "Aye, my grandfather was married twice and some claimed the marriage to my grandmother was invalid. But it was solved by a Papal dispensation. It is...nonsense."

"Not if you were dead. Then Atholl could claim the throne as the rightful heir!" Joan wrung her hands. "Who would support a child king against such a claim? Any more than they fought for you when Albany was regent. And a child—and, James, a child is easy to kill."

"By the Rood, this is madness."

"Myrton thinks that the true power behind the plot are Atholl's grandson, who will be his heir, and that foul Robert Graham. And others he thinks support them. Crawford, for one, and some churchmen. Those you could handle, but James, you are in great danger here if an English force attacks. They could send ships up the Clyde whilst an army from

Cumberland came up by the West March. Then you would be cut off from all aid."

"I must see strong evidence before I believe it is Atholl. He has supported me well...has been loyal. But Graham. Aye, his hatred is poisonous. Crawford. Aye, he as well hates me. There are others who have reason to want to see an end to my laws. To see a weak crown that they can rule."

She put her hand softly on his arm. "Myrton confessed he had no evidence of who was behind the plot, but the plot is clear, that some in your army plan to betray you."

James sat on the edge of the table gripping it with his fingers so hard they went numb. Panting with rage, he said every curse word he knew. Joan flinched but stood silent until he had worked through his fury. Finally he said, "Forgive me, love." He shook his head. "They leave me no choice. If I'm to deal with an insurrection, I cannae do so here. I must break off the siege. God damn them! They'll say I lifted it from fear, but I can't allow myself to be cut off. And I must put an investigation in motion to find the truth of these accusations. But Atholl part of such a plot? I cannae believe that. Am I cursed? Only enemies all around?"

Joan slipped her arm around his waist and laid her head on his shoulder. "Don't say that. You are well loved."

He sighed. "We must return to Edinburgh forthwith."

Chapter Twenty-Seven

DECEMBER 1436

Dark clouds ran before the wind, and fine snowflakes stung James' cheeks. The water of the Forth stirred. Waves sent plumes to wash over the rocky bank. The damp edges of his wool cloak clung to his thighs as he sat ahorse. He glanced at Joan at his side. She gave him a wry smile and shrugged, tugging her fur cloak tighter around her neck.

The guards shifted miserably in the saddle, and Sir David Dunbar gave an audible sigh. Although it was only a little after Terce, Queensbury was silent in the December chill. Even the village dogs didn't bother to bark at them. Houses had their shutters fastened against the wind, which carried away streams of smoke that leaked from chimneys and thatched roofs. The wind rattled the branches of the trees and made the reeds along the bank of the River Forth bend low.

Suddenly hands latched onto his foot in the stirrup; James flinched and his horse sidled, snorting. He looked down at what had grabbed hold of him: little more than a bundle of rags with a baked face.

"Hoi! Loose His Grace!" one of the guards shouted. Another waved his hands about shouting, "Away with you."

The old woman looked up at James with eyes like wounds. She clung onto his stirrup and cried, "My Lord King, ye must hear me!"

Joan caught his eye and gave her head a little shake. His lips twitched. "What's to do? Speak then."

"My king, an ye pass this water, ye shall never return again alive."

Robert Stewart, his new chamberlain, crowded her with his horse. "Away with you, hag. Leave the king be."

"Wait." James waved Stewart back and leaned sideways, looking more closely at her. "What do you mean? Why shall I never return alive?"

James supposed Stewart had frightened the old wifey, for she clung even more tightly to his stirrup. He breathed out an exasperated breath. With the rebellion at Roxburgh and Robert Graham in hiding, it was just slightly possible she had heard something he should know. Myrton still believed that others besides Graham had been behind the plot. James wished he had evidence of it. No one who came to him could be ignored. He tried once more. "What is it you want to tell me?"

"Go back," the woman wailed. "Ye shall die if ye go on."

"Who told you I would die?" He tried to make his voice gentle.

"Huthart," she said, "Huthart said so." She turned and ran, rags swirling around her.

"Just an old madwoman," Stewart said.

James looked at the men around him. "Huthart? Does anyone know that name?" He considered sending someone after the old thing, but the bow of the ferry bumped against the dock, and black-robed friars who ran it hurled looped lines over piling. In a moment they bowed to the king. James nudged his mount, and they sloshed toward wide craft to cross the Firth of Forth and ride for Perth. It was nothing.

Chapter Twenty-Eight

FEBRUARY 20, 1437

A fire crackled on the hearth of the monastery guest house, giving off the scent of oak. Branches of candles and a glowing brazier brightened the hall and helped keep out the chill. Joan settled in a chair beside the hearth with a sigh of satisfaction. One of the squires was plucking a melody on a lute as a new knight's page, young Walter Straiton, helped himself to a sweetmeat still on a tray from dinner. The king hummed faintly under his breath as he bent his head over a chessboard. The Earl of Angus nodded over his wine, and Robert Lauder sprawled lazily in a chair.

In the corridor a door slammed. Sir David Dunbar came in stomping his feet and shook a few flakes of snow from his cloak. He bowed first to Joan and then to the king. He handed over a missive from the Papal Nuncio biding in the Kirk whilst in Perth since there was no room in Blackfriars Monastery where they stayed. James glowered at the missive.

"Business so late?" Joan frowned. She had worked trying to distract James these last weeks through Christmastide and Hogmanay, and at last he seemed more himself.

He eyed the chessboard before him before he flicked open the seal with his thumb. "Only a moment." He scanned it quickly and tossed it aside. "I believe the Nuncio and I will come to an agreement between us soon over my disagreement with the Holy Father, but first we must await the chancellor to arrive."

On the other side of the board, Alexander MacDonald used a broad, tanned finger to push a bishop to a new position. "It has been much too pleasant an evening for The King's Grace to think about business of state." He grinned. "There will always be more business anon."

Sir David laughed. "I have to tell you! That old witch woman from the ferry is now crying and moaning at the doors that there is death loose in the night."

"That old hag?" Robert Stewart said. "She should be flogged for blethering such tales."

Joan gave Stewart a cool look. James said they had found no evidence that his new Chamberlain and Atholl, Robert's grandfather, were part of the plot against him, but Joan couldn't like him. Or trust him. James said old Atholl did not treat Robert kindly. Graham had disappeared into hiding, and James had replaced the Keepers at Dumbarton Castle and Stirling Castle. Atholl had sworn he had no part in any sedition, but now Joan looked at the young man and wondered.

"No need to treat her harshly. I shall see her in the morn." James gave MacDonald a wry look. "A certain lady bandied it about that you are the King of Love," he grinned, "and the old wifey says that a king will be slain in this land. Since there are no kings here but you and me, you had best beware. For I give my oath to the saints, I am under your kinghood in the service of Love."

Alexander snorted and shook his head. Joan held her hand over her mouth as she laughed. Alexander was indeed a King of Love with all of the ladies.

The king made another move on the board. "I have you, my lord," he said, chuckling with triumph.

Alexander rose. "I yield, Sire, and shall retire for the night. One day I'll best you, though. I give you my word."

Joan rose from her seat at the card table, yawning, "I shall retire as well."

She smiled when she saw James yawn after her. They'd had a quiet winter's evening of song, card playing, and chess. There wasn't enough room in the monastery for most of the court, so they had it nearly to themselves, a rare bit of near privacy she always relished when in Perth, so different from being crowded together in a castle.

She stretched her back and called to Catherine Douglas to come undress her. "A good night to you all," she said. "Will you join me soon, Sire?"

"Soon, my lady." James rose as well. He waved away his squire. "David, I'm not yet so fat I cannae unfasten my hose. Hie to your own bed in town."

Angus and Lauder were bidding the king a good night as they bowed, moving towards the door, also being lodged in the town. "I'll see to the doors and the guards," she heard Robert Stewart say as she left. Catherine Douglas scooped up her wooly lapdog from where it snoozed to follow. Joan strolled through the king's dressing room and into the inner chamber. The large room, walls covered with Flemish tapestries of nobles picnicking and at the hunt and deerskin rungs on the floor, was a pleasant retreat. Agnes Gray gave a deep curtsey before she went back to folding clothes at one of the wardrobes.

As she unlaced Joan's gown, Catherine Douglas said, "His Grace seems happier, less upset now."

"Shhhh." Joan pressed a finger to her lips. James would certainly not be happy to hear her discussing him with her lady-in-waiting, but Catherine was right. For the first time since the debacle at the siege of Roxburgh, James seemed to be enjoying himself. He was always happier in the less martial setting of Blackfriars.

Catherine slipped Joan into her robe and was chatting idly about when they might leave for Linlithgow Palace and what the children might be up to in Edinburgh.

As she was loosening Joan's hair, James opened the door. He said to Walter, "Bring up a flagon of wine from the cellar, lad, and then you may retire for the night."

He'd changed from his clothes into a furred bedrobe and warm slippers. He came to kiss her cheek and she sat for Catherine to brush out her hair. James wasn't the only one who was feeling happier than he had been in a long while. She smiled up at him. "We could bide at Blackfriars for time, do you not think, James?"

He went to hold his hands out to the fire, popping away on the hearth. "For a time, if you like. I'm in no great hurry to travel in the snow. David said that it's covered the ground."

When she turned her head to watch him before the fire, she laughed. "Speaking of covering, close your robe, if you please. I swear that no longer covers you at all. That is more than I'd have my ladies viewing."

James patted his belly before he pulled his robe tighter around himself, grinning. "God's mercy, I'm no longer a stripling, woman. A man grows a bit of meat on him as he ages."

She shook her head, still chuckling. It had been a while since things had been so light in their household. "I've no complaint about that, James, but pray do not display it quite so readily to my ladies."

"Indeed, I try very hard not to peek, my lady," Catherine said with a distinct smile in her voice.

"And that is why you—" Joan turned at a crash that came from the hallway. "What was..."

She stood up and stared at the door. At some distance, there was shouting and the distinctive sound of the clanking of armor. James turned his head, listening intently. Those were not sounds you should hear in a monastery at night.

Joan opened her mouth to say they should call for the guards when there were crashes that sounded like fighting. From only a short distance Walter Straiton shouted, "Treason! Sire! Flee!" Walter's voice rose to a high-pitched scream and was cut off.

Catherine ran to the door to bar it. "Holy Mary, the bar is gone." She turned to lean back against the door, her eyes wide with terror. A bar usually hung by a chain next to the door.

Joan pressed her hand to her chest. Her heart was beating so hard she felt as though she must hold it in. But there was no time for weakness. "Where are the guards?"

"Lured away mayhap." James turned slowly, his hands grasping and ungrasping as though desperate for the feel of a weapon.

Joan ran to grab James' arm and pull him to the window. "Flee, love. Run."

He started to protest but she cut him off. "They won't harm me if you're not here. It has to be you they are after."

In a stride James was at the windows. He ripped open the shutters. Joan peered out beside him and through the snow flurries, the light of half a dozen torches lit the courtyard. They showed men, perhaps a dozen, fully armed from the glitter of the torchlight on steel.

"Aye, if I'm here they may kill you as well as me." He grabbed her shoulder. "Whatever happens, reach James. They'll go after him next."

She shook her head and looked desperately around the room, and then pointed at the floor. The drain. It was something you would never find in a castle, but in Blackfriars', years ago when having the rugs beaten, she'd spotted a trapdoor that led to drains, apparently long unused. She turned and pointed to a small table. "Catherine, Agnes, push that in front of the door. Anything you can find to delay them."

James grabbed the edge of the deerskin rug and dragged it away. He dropped to his knees and used his fingertips to prise open the trapdoor. She leaned, peering down. It was a long drop, considerably farther than she was tall.

He grabbed her and pressed a kiss to her temple. "I shall rouse the guards and bring help."

"Hurry! Oh, hurry!" she wrung her hands. There should be something more she could do. Something!

James lowered himself over, hung for a moment by his hands, and dropped. Joan started to tell him to run, but the door shook under someone's pounding. Catherine and Agnes had shoved the table in front of it, but that wouldn't keep them out. She struggled to lift the heavy oaken trapdoor. It dropped into place with a crash. Catherine ran to help her pull the rugs over it.

Outwith the door there were curses, a thud against the heavy wood, and it flew open, the table scraping from the force. Joan stepped onto the rug, both hands pressed to her chest. She could feel her whole body trembling. Sir Robert Graham stumbled into the room throwing his full weight at the door, a bloody sword in his hand. Behind him, Joan saw Robert Stewart. Behind them four more men.

"You!" she gasped at Robert Stewart.

"Aye. The new heir to the throne after we finish this night's work."

"Where is the tyrant? The murderer?" Graham demanded. "James Stewart. Where is he?"

Joan pressed her mouth into a straight line and tried to still her trembling.

Graham ran to poke under the bed, kicked Catherine's

yapping lapdog out of the way. He threw open the shutters and called down, asking if they had seen anything. Then he whirled and strode to her. "Where is he?"

When she shook her head, he pulled back his arm and thrust his sword through her shoulder. She opened her mouth to scream, but the pain took away her voice. But she heard Agnes's shrieks.

She was somehow on the floor, although she didn't remember falling, and rolled over to crawl, but when she moved her stomach roiled. Blood dripped into a crimson pool on the floor. Then Catherine was lifting her. She ripped off her veil and wadded to press to the wound.

"Why did you do that?" Robert Stewart asked.

"You think we dare risk letting them live to tell the tale?" Graham demanded. He grabbed Catherine by the arm, jerked her to her feet, and backhanded her. "Where is he? Where?"

Joan watched desperately as Catherine shook her head. "I dinnae ken. He ran out of the chamber. How could I ken where he is now?"

Graham shoved her away. "How could he have slipped past us? He has to be here somewhere." He strode out the door, cloak flapping behind him, the others tramping after him.

Catherine ran to the wardrobe, grabbed handkerchiefs, and knelt, stuffing them against the bloody wound in Joan's shoulder. "Graham means to kill us all," she whispered.

A clatter from below the rug made Joan flinch. There was another as though someone tossed a stone at the trapdoor. "Mercy on us, it's James." Joan motioned to Agnes, who was kneeling beside the bed, hands clutched against her mouth. "Agnes, close the door!"

The girl lurched to her feet and scurried to softly push the door closed. Catherine grabbed the rug and pulled it aside.

She prised at the trapdoor and grunted. "Come help, girl," she demanded.

Agnes was whimpering with fear, but she hurried over and knelt, and between the two of them, grunting, they managed to open it. A wave of stale air wafted out.

"The way out is closed," James called up. "And I cannae reach the edge to pull up. Tie sheets together and tie them to the bed post. If I can reach my armor...my weapons...then we have a chance. Hurry before they return."

Joan's shoulder seared with pain as she pressed the wad of cloth to it. Already they were soggy with blood, but she pushed herself to her knees. "The ones on the bed. Strip it!"

As Catherine knotted one end to a bedpost and Agnes knotted it to another sheet, James called up, "Was it Graham? I could not tell the voices through the floor."

"Yes, Graham," Joan said. "And Robert Stewart. His son. Those two brothers who are his friends, the Halls..."

"It's tied!" Agnes jumped up. Her feet skidded in the pool of blood and she shrieked. Catherine lunged for her but wasn't close enough. The girl tumbled into the opening and shrieked again as she fell. Catherine dashed for the trapdoor and strained to lift it, managing to lift it halfway.

Stewart dashed in. "He's down here!" Robert Stewart crowed. "We have him trapped." He gave Catherine a buffet. The trapdoor crashed open.

Joan pressed her hand to her mouth to keep from begging. Stewart dropped down into the dark mouth of the tunnel. James shouted, "Curse you!" There was a smack of a blow and a grunt. She heard a thud as though someone hit the wall of the drain. She almost sobbed as she remembered seeing James throw a man when he wrestled. There was another loud bang and a man's angry shout.

Hall and his brother ran and dropped into a crouch to let

themselves down. Joan crawled to the trapdoor and leaned her head down to try to see, but it was black as pitch. There were grunts and the sound of blows.

A shadow fell across her. She looked up in time to see Graham's iron-shod foot aimed at her side. Automatically, she tried to dodge, but the blow knocked her across to the wall. He knelt, put one hand on the floor, and jumped into the hole.

Below, another man grunted from a blow Then there was a horrible moist sound, and then another and another, one after another and another. James screamed, "Misericordia, Deus!"

Graham laughed, sounding almost hysterical. "He's begging for mercy. The tyrant!"

The traitorous fool didn't care that James was praying. She stuffed her fingers in her mouth to keep in the scream of anger and pain. They were killing him! Mother of Mercy, let this be a nightmare.

There was a choked cry that died away with a bubbling sound. Catherine pulled Joan's arm around her shoulder. Putting her arm around Joan's waist, she hauled her to her feet. "They may not be watching the kitchen door. We must flee."

Joan stared at her for a second and turned to look at the gaping maw of the trapdoor. James. Then she remembered, "Oh, Blessed Virgin! The children." Her legs wobbled as Catherine half dragged her through the hallway, into the commodious kitchen, the fire in the hearth banked. She could feel blood dripping between her breasts under her robe. The door opened into the garden instead of the courtyard; they lurched between the bare rows. The Chapterhouse was a dark bulk in the blowing snow, but monks would be of no aid. The flurries melted on her wet face, so she could pretend that she wasn't crying. But every breath was a silent scream of rage. She had to reach the Nuncio. There, safe, she could find help.

The gate through the paling fence onto the lane squealed as it opened. Joan flinched at the noise, but they stumbled on through the slush. Suddenly, a group emerged from the darkness in front of them. A sob ripped her throat. They were caught, she feared, as the shapes rushed towards them. Then in the flickering light of a torch she recognized David Dunbar, his doublet unfastened and hair wild, but the light caught on the sword in his hand. Behind him were two gate guards in ill-fitting mail.

Dunbar shouted, "It's the queen!" He ran to her and dropped to one knee. "Your Grace..." He was almost gabbling in distress. "You're hurt..."

"The king." Joan felt as though her throat was closing up, so she must force the words out. Catherine held her up as Joan gasped out, "Robert Stewart betrayed us. No guards. And Graham. They...they've..." She pointed behind them. "Murdered..."

Dunbar leapt to his feet and whirled to the gate guards. "The Nuncio at St. John's Kirk. Escort the queen to him." He pointed toward Blackfriars with his sword. "Send help to me there! But I cannae wait."

He pelted the way Joan had come, toward the monastery. The torch light gleamed in the guards' horrified eyes. One bobbed an awkward bow and reached for her but then jerked back.

"Why are we standing here?" Catherine snapped. She tightened her arm around Joan's waist, and they began to hobble toward the Kirk. The silent one lifted the torch higher as he led the way, whilst his companion hefted his cudgel, looking to and fro as they went.

Joan shook with chills. She couldn't feel her hands. Her

legs were leaden as she struggled to take a step and then another. The torchlight blurred and faded out. A man's voice, sounding as though it were underwater, said, "Let me carry her, my lady. We must hurry." Then Joan was floating. She let the blackness suck her under where there was no grief.

Chapter Twenty-Nine

❧❦❧

A voice was screaming. A boyish terrified screaming. One of the pages...

"James!" They must flee, but he was not here. She threw back the bed hangings and ran desperately to throw open the doors of the wardrobes. "James!" she called. "James, where are you?" He didn't answer. "Guards! Someone. Help me." She heard the march of footsteps outside and the gurgling last breath of a dying boy. They are coming. They are coming for me. She ran to the door, panting with panic, pounding on it to get out. The room grew dark. The light has gone out of Scotland. "James, help me."

"Your Grace! My lady. Can you hear me? You're safe."

Wait. She knew that woman's voice. What was happening? What...?

"Madam, you are all right." Now the voice sounded desperate. "You are safe now. Wake up."

The mad phantasmagoria of dream and memory shattered. She was in a strange bed, but that was Catherine Douglas's voice calling to her over and over. The disembodied voice sounded despairing.

Her eyes fluttered open. She was wrapped in warm wool and the room was in watery daylight. Her shoulder throbbed, and when tried to turn in the soft bed, it seemed to be pierced by a hot knife.

"Your Grace." A branch of candles appeared and the familiar face of the Earl of Douglas was staring down at her.

"Douglas," she croaked.

"The king..." His throat worked and his plain face was drawn up like a fist. He crossed himself. "He lies in the Charterhouse."

She managed a nod. Her mouth was too parched to speak; her tongue clove to the roof of her mouth. "Water."

Catherine lifted her shoulders carefully, although Joan had to bite back a moan, and put a cup to her lips. She took a long swallow, licked her lips, and sipped again. "Douglas, the children. You must go. Hurry! If any try to come between you and my son—" She gulped down a sob. "—cut them down."

He bowed his head for a moment before he took her hand and kissed it. He jumped to his feet, and she turned her head to watch him stride from the room. She closed her eyes. If only this could be a bad dream, a terrible nightmare. But it was not, so she opened them and said to Catherine, "Dunbar, he went to pursue the traitors. What happened?"

"Injured, Your Grace, but he lives."

Joan tried to sit up. She fought through the pain to swing her legs over the edge of the bed. "Bring the Earl of Angus to me. He must pursue Robert Stewart and the others, take them prisoner. Where is the Earl of March? He shall seize the Earl of Atholl. All of them traitors. Murderers! They must be returned to for punishment." Oh, she would see they were punished. She crossed herself and softly uttered an oath that they would scream their way to their deaths. "And then dress me. I must..." A sob built up beneath her ribs. She shoved a fist against her mouth and breathed roughly through her nose until she could speak. "I must go to my husband."

Epilogue
MARCH 26, 1437

A tern circled overhead as Joan made her way toward the gallery she'd had built. She glanced down at her son thoughtfully. But he kept his back straight and his chin high. His clothes were all crimson, patterned with lions rampant, a child-sized gold crown on his head. If the crown weighed heavily on him, he did not complain. Around them, the guards in the royal livery were grim faced, their pikes in white knuckled hands.

Across the city, church bells began to toll.

Ahead, two guards shouted, "Make way! Make way for the king!" Beyond the guards, the whole city was moving, all rushing to see the final punishment of the leader of the traitors. The bells grew louder, clanging, clamoring. Joan bit her lip, her shoulder throbbing with every step, for the wound had festered and was only slowly healing.

Around them excited voices shouted.

"...Earl of Atholl. I got him with a rotten turnip yesterday when he was in the pillory!"

"I heard he died of the pelting."

"Nae."

By the time Joan climbed the steps of the gallery, people were packed shoulder to shoulder. The market square was a solid mass of people all yammering and prodding with shoulder and elbow to get closer to the scaffold, topped by a long table, raised in the middle. She briefly touched James' shoulder. His face was as pale as whey so that the birthmark on his cheek showed as crimson as a splash of dark wine. The bells were so loud her ears rang with it.

That was when she saw Walter Stewart, Earl of Atholl.

He stood at the foot of the scaffold, supported between two guards. He wore a blue velvet doublet and an iron crown on his head. A dark bruise stained one cheek and an eye was swollen shut. He was more being held erect than standing. A priest stood behind him, beads clutched in hand and head bent, his lips moving in prayer.

A long line of liveried pikemen held back the crowd.

Atholl shook loose from the guards beside him and stolidly climbed the steps of the pillory. When he reached the top, the bells ceased to toll and slowly quiet descended over the square. He turned and swept a look across the crowd, and began to speak, his voice thin and hoarse. "I am Walter Stewart—last living son of King Robert the second." He raised his voice and continued. "I am the rightful King of Scots! We killed the usurper!"

The crowd began to scream and yell. Boos, hisses, and curses filled the air. A stone soared out of the crowd and hit him in the chest. A guard grabbed his arm to keep him upright and another stepped in front of the earl. More stones followed that clattered like hail on the scaffold. A thousand voices were shouting. Robert Keith, the Marischal stepped out from behind the ranks of the guards, raising both hands for quiet. "The Earl of Atholl signed his confession to treason and murder, has further condemned himself with his own words. Now keep your peace whilst we carry out our duty. His treason shall not go unpunished."

The crowd bellowed.

Keith drew his dirk from his belt and used it to rip Atholl's clothes from his pale, stringy body. Atholl stared blank faced over the Marischal's head. The guards moved aside as the executioner strode forward, all in black, doublet, hose, and hood. The roar of the throng was like the sea crashing over Joan, thundering in her ears. She put a hand on James' thin shoulder and squeezed.

High atop the scaffold the executioner gestured, and the naked earl was hoisted onto the table. He lifted a knife above the Earl's belly.

Joan choked out a soft, "You may close your eyes if you want, Jamie."

"No." James looked up at her, his mouth in a thin, determined line. "He murdered my father."

Faintly, as if from far away, when the knife descended, Joan heard Atholl scream.

Also by J R Tomlin

The Stewart Chronicle

- A King Ensnared

Standalone Prequel to the Black Douglas Trilogy

- Freedom's Sword

The Black Douglas Trilogy

- A Kingdom's Cost
- Countenance of War
- Not for Glory

The Sir Law Kintour Mysteries

- The Templar's Cross
- The Winter Kill
- The Intelligencer

For more information about my novels and a free offer, please visit my website at jrtomlin.com.

Author's Notes

The research for *A King Ensnared* and *A King Uncaged* was very considerable. I kept as much as possible to documented facts given the requirements of telling a story. There are few books that are very well researched about King James I of Scotland. My own re-telling of the story of his life is based upon Volume 8 of Walter Bower's Scotichronicon which is available in translation, *The dethe of James Kynge of Scotis* which unfortunately for most readers is not available in translation, and E. W. M. Balfour-Melville's excellent *James I, King of Scots*. However, I also had reference to many other documents, and of course, at times simply drew what seemed to me to be the most logical conclusion from available evidence.

In writing historical fiction, an author sometimes must choose between making the language understandable and making it authentic. While I use modern English in this novel, the people of fifteenth-century Scotland spoke mainly Scots, Gaelic, and French. To give at least a feel of their language and because some concepts can only be expressed using phrases no longer in common use, there are Scottish and archaic English words in this work, particularly in the

AUTHOR'S NOTES

dialogue. Some are close to or even identical to current English although used in a medieval context. The following is a list of terms in which I explain some of the words and usages that might be unfamiliar. I hope you will find the list interesting and useful.

List of Principal Historical Characters

- James I, King of Scots
- Joan Beaufort—Queen Consort of King James I, daughter of John Beaufort, Earl of Somerset and niece of King Henry IV of England
- Archibald Douglas—Earl of Wigtoun and later Earl of Douglas
- Walter Stewart—Earl of Atholl, son of Robert II of Scotland and half uncle of King James I
- Henry Percy—Earl of Northumberland
- Henry Wardlaw—Bishop of St. Andrews, primate of Scotland
- Sir Robert Lauder of Edrington—Lord of Bass Rock Castle
- William Lauder—Bishop of Glasgow, Chancellor of Scotland
- William Giffard—Esquire of the Tower of London
- Murdoch Stewart—Duke of Albany
- Walter Stewart—Eldest son and heir of the Duke of Albany
- John the Fat—(actually he was called James the

LIST OF PRINCIPAL HISTORICAL CHARACTERS

Fat, but a superfluity of Jameses led me to use the name John in the novel) Youngest son of the Duke of Albany
- Alexander Stewart—Son of the Duke of Albany
- John Lyon—Priest and secretary to James Stewart
- Dougal Drummond—Priest and confessor to James Stewart
- Alexander Stewart—Earl of Mar, illegitimate son of Alexander Stewart, known as the Wolf of Badenoch
- Robert Stewart—Grandson of the Earl of Atholl
- Sir Robert Graham of Kinpont—Scottish knight and landowner
- John Cameron—Secretary to King James I, later Bishop of Glasgow and Chancellor of Scotland
- William Douglas—Earl of Angus
- Alexander MacDonald—Earl of Ross also known as Lord of the Isles

Glossary

- Afeart (Scots) — Afraid.
- Ain (Scots) — Own.
- Any road — anyway.
- Aright — In a proper manner; correctly.
- Auld (Scots) — Old.
- Aye — Yes.
- Bailey — An enclosed courtyard within the walls of a castle.
- Bairn (Scots), Child.
- Bannock (Scots) — Unleavened flatbread bread made of oatmeal or barley flour, generally cooked on a flat metal sheet.
- Barbican — A tower or other fortification, especially one at a gate or drawbridge.
- Battlement — A parapet in which rectangular gaps occur at intervals to allow for firing arrows.
- Bedeck — To adorn or ornament in a showy fashion.
- Betime — On occasion.
- Bracken — Weedy fern.

GLOSSARY

- Brae (Scots) — Hill or slope.
- Braeside (Scots) — Hillside.
- Barmy — Daft.
- Braw (Scots), Fine or excellent.
- Buffet — A blow or cuff with or as if with the hand.
- Burn (Scots) — Watercourses from large streams to small rivers.
- Cannae (Scots) — cannot
- Chivvied — Harassed.
- Cloying — Causing distaste or disgust by supplying with too much of something originally pleasant.
- Churl — A peasant.
- Cot — Small building.
- Couched — To lower (a lance, for example) to a horizontal position.
- Courser — A swift, strong horse, often used as a warhorse.
- Crenel — An open space or notch between two merlons in the battlement of a castle or city wall.
- Crook — Tool, such as a bishop's crosier or a shepherd's staff.
- Curtain wall — The defensive outer wall of a medieval castle.
- Curst — A past tense and a past participle of curse.
- Defile — A narrow gorge or pass.
- Destrier — The heaviest class of warhorse.
- Din — A jumble of loud, usually discordant sounds.
- Dirk — A long, straight-bladed dagger.
- Dinnae (Scots) — does not.
- Dower — The part or interest of a deceased man's real estate allotted by law to his widow for her

GLOSSARY

lifetime, often applied to property brought to the marriage by the bride.
- Erstwhile — In the past, at a former time, formerly.
- Faggot, A bundle of sticks or twigs, esp. when bound together and used as fuel.
- Falchion — A short, broad sword with a convex cutting edge and a sharp point.
- Farrier — One who shoes horses.
- Fash — Annoy.
- Forbye — Besides.
- Garderobe, A privy chamber.
- Git — A bastard or fool.
- Glen — A valley.
- Gorse — A spiny yellow-flowered European shrub.
- Groat — An English silver coin worth four pence.
- Hallo — A variant of "hello."
- Hart — A male deer.
- Haugh (Scots) — A low-lying meadow in a river valley.
- Hie — To go quickly; hasten.
- Hodden-grey — coarse homespun cloth produced in Scotland made by mixing black and white wools.
- Holy Rood (Scots) — The Holy Cross.
- Jesu — Vocative form of Jesus.
- Ken — To know (a person or thing).
- Kirtle — A woman's dress typically worn over a chemise or smock.
- Laying — To engage energetically in an action.
- Loch — Lake or narrow arm of the sea.
- Louring — Angry or sullen.
- Malmsey — A sweet fortified Madeira wine.
- Marischal — The hereditary custodian of the

GLOSSARY

Royal Regalia of Scotland and protector of the king's person.
- Maudlin — Effusively or tearfully sentimental.
- Mawkish — Excessively and objectionably sentimental.
- Mercies — Without any protection against; helpless before.
- Merlon — A solid portion between two crenels in a battlement or crenellated wall.
- Midge — A gnat-like fly found worldwide and frequently occurring in swarms near ponds and lakes, prevalent across Scotland in certain seasons.
- Mien — Bearing or manner, especially as it reveals an inner state of mind.
- Mount — Mountain or hill.
- Murk — Darkness or thick mist.
- Nae — No, not.
- Nave — The central approach to a church's high altar; the main body of the church.
- Nock — To fit an arrow to a bowstring.
- Nook — Hidden or secluded spot.
- Outwith (Scots) — Outside, beyond.
- Palfrey — A placid saddle horse used for ordinary riding.
- Pap — Material lacking real value or substance.
- Parapet — A defensive wall, usually with a walk, above which the wall is chest to head high.
- Pate — Head or brain.
- Perfidy — The act or an instance of treachery.
- Pillion — Pad or cushion behind the saddle for a passenger or riding on such a cushion.
- Piebald — Spotted or patched.
- Privily — Privately or secretly.

GLOSSARY

- Quintain — Object mounted on a post, used as a target in tilting exercises.
- Rood — Crucifix.
- Runnel — A narrow channel.
- Saddlebow, The arched upper front part of a saddle.
- Saltire — An ordinary in the shape of a Saint Andrew's cross; when capitalized, the flag of Scotland (a white saltire on a blue field).
- Samite — A heavy silk fabric, often interwoven with gold or silver.
- Sassenach (Scots) — An Englishman, derived from the Scots Gaelic Sasunnach meaning, originally, "Saxon."
- Seneschal — A steward or major-domo.
- Shite — Shit.
- Siller (Scots) — Silver.
- Sirrah — Mister; fellow. Used as a contemptuous form of address.
- Sleekit (Scots) — Unctuous, sly, crafty.
- Sumpter — Pack animal, such as a horse or mule.
- Surcoat — An outer tunic often worn over armor.
- Tail — A noble's following of guards.
- Tisane — An herbal infusion drunk as a beverage or for its mildly medicinal effect.
- Trencher — A plate or platter for food, often a thick slice of stale bread.
- Trestle table — A table made up of two or three trestle supports over which a tabletop is placed.
- Trews — Close-fitting trousers.
- Tun — Large cask for liquids, especially wine.
- Wain — Open farm wagon.
- Wattle — A fleshy, wrinkled, often brightly colored fold of skin hanging from the neck.

GLOSSARY

- Westering — To move westward.
- Wheedling — Using flattery or cajolery to achieve one's ends.
- Whilst — While.
- Whisht — To be silent—often used as an interjection to urge silence.
- Wroth — Angry

Made in the USA
Middletown, DE
08 January 2020